THE GRAVE DIGGERS
Grave Diggers Series

- Book 1 -

by
Chris Fritschi

The Grave Diggers
by
Chris Fritschi

Copyright © 2016 by Chris Fritschi

V4

ISBN:
ISBN-13:

Click or visit
chrisfritschi.com

DISCLAIMER

This is a work of fiction. Names, characters, businesses, places, events and incidents are either the products of the author's imagination or used in a fictitious manner. Any resemblance to actual persons, living or dead, or actual events is purely coincidental.

This book is dedicated to my wife for her tireless support and encouragement.

ACKNOWLEDGMENTS

A special thanks to all of you, you know who you are, for the encouragement and finger wagging that kept me on my toes through the development of this book. The critical, but honest, input from my beta-readers Cinnamon, Kevin, Samantha, Lauren and my wholly unbiased wife, Karen, shed light on areas where the book needed fixing. You guys make me look good.

My thanks to my friend, Mark, for his helpful suggestions. Enough can't be said for my wife who spent endless hours listening to me brain-dump over this book. Her patience and support never flagged.

PROLOGUE

A New World

O nce the sole heirs of eternal rest, the dead rejected their inheritance and swept down upon man, woman and child in a mindless horror.

In some places of the world they had no warning. It spawned out of the darkness, and the ones caught off guard were wiped out. Maybe they were lucky. In other places, there were warnings something was coming, but they were ill prepared for the enormity and speed of it.

The largest killer was panic. Whole cities imploded on themselves, weeks before any sign of the devouring horror appeared. Murder, looting, hoarding; nearly every conceivable variation of sectarianism to justify the brutality one human being could execute upon another was carried out in the name of racial superiority, religious right, the greater good, even humanity, but it all came down to 'better them than me'.

Ironically enough, the 'tin foil hat' crowd and survivalists did better than others, and hunkered down in their fortified homes, lairs, or bunkers.

The outbreak plumed across the face of the Earth. Infection was the favorite word of the spin-doctors, but few people bought into that, and those foolish enough, or unwilling to believe the reality of what was happening, tried to treat their 'sick' loved ones. Their mistake was short lived, and only added to the mounting millions of walking death.

For whatever misguided reasons, a few governments, leaders and politicians played it down using euphemisms, causing further confusion. The grisly truth was that corpses were cannibalizing the human population.

Perhaps the leading cause of pointless deaths was the United Nations. Countries were losing ground and people to the growing onslaught, and attempted to selectively eliminate the threat in areas where a population, living and undead, were tightly intermingled, by carpet-bombing entire towns. Wanting to save lives, but without offering a solution, the U.N. stepped in and threatened severe sanctions of food, medicines, and aid, unless the offending governments ceased their 'inhumane genocide'; a decision that only allowed the ranks of ravaging dead to swell.

France, Italy, and Spain were the loudest critics of the "senseless murder" of human life, and chose to set the example of the humane way to deal with his outbreak. All three countries were on the brink of being swallowed up in less than two months. It was enough to convince them to change their position from "senseless murder" to "survival", and they mobilized their military. After that, the remaining countries told the U.N. they could shove their collective sanctions, and unleashed every conventional weapon they had at their disposal.

In the United States, hard decisions had to be made to save many at the sacrifice of the few. The Federal Clean Border Act worked on the same principle of amputating an infected limb to save the rest of the body. Areas that were judged too far gone were closed off, or destroyed. There was resistance to the plan, based on past failures of government plans. Their concerns soon became justified; the short notice of the border locations and the 'cut off' time people had to reach them resulted in fewer than 25 percent arriving in time. As losses began mounting, the local governments took things into their own hands. Units of the National Guard were activated, but they couldn't bring enough forces to the fight.

Projected losses were grim until the President held an emergency State of the Union address, where she announced a temporary suspension of all civilian gun control laws. The President made it clear she was calling on the citizens to help save their country, but would not condone lawlessness. To drive that home, she announced that law enforcement and military personal had been authorized to "shoot on sight" anyone caught committing capital crimes, robbery, or looting. People, who before had chosen to defend their homes, began to come out. At first it was only a few here and there, but eventually momentum grew and the National Guard had more help than they knew what to do with.

Major cities were able to wipe out the undead long enough to erect fortifications. In the end, the US was for the most part, safe. From time to time, Costal Defense would catch a stray one that made its way from who knows where. Eventually, America settled into a skittish stability.

While some countries were hanging by their fingernails, they were at least hanging. South America never had a chance. The rest of the world was fighting for survival, and the aid South America did receive it was too little, too late.

In a staggering cascade, one country after another fell as the continent was overrun. In many cases, governments were abandoned more than they collapsed. Left with no leadership, or structure of any kind, it was in the hands of each individual whether they lived or died. Masses of people swarmed the harbors, airports, and train stations, but it was like spitting on a forest fire; with no way out they packed together ever tighter. Then the undead came, and the carnage was apocalyptic. It was the most horrific and tragic event the world had ever known.

Desperation drove thousands to the ocean, grabbing anything that would float and walking into the sea with no other thought than to escape. Bodies of the drowned began washing up on shores all over the world, most along the coast of Africa and as far as Australia. Of an estimated population of 380 million, less than a quarter escaped with their lives. Of those, only ten percent survived to make it to another country.

Not all died at the hands of the undead. When the global community saw South America was entirely lost, Uruguay and the eastern coast of Argentina were decimated by multiple nuclear strikes. Some speculated the attacks were made in the desperate hope that others would follow suit and scorch the continent clean.

Whatever the reason, those responsible for the nuclear attacks were never discovered, and the attacks only pushed the future of the human race closer to the edge of extinction. Accusations and threats flew between countries, and with many of them vulnerable and weakened came the fear of a full-out nuclear war breaking out.

In the end, it was announced that the source of the attack could not accurately be determined. The United States claimed their satellites had been down for maintenance during that time, and didn't see the 'plume signatures' of any warhead launches. Russia also admitted their satellite was inoperable due to a sizable solar flare.

As the fear of retaliation eased, attention turned back on South America and the threat it posed. As countries were beginning to make meager gains in staunching the horror spreading around them, there was a real worry South America could be the source of a sequel to this historic nightmare. Discussions sprang up regarding what to do. The problem was any talk of a nuclear option instantly started finger pointing and dangerous accusations about the first attack. South America was shaping up to be a political stalemate that could go on for years.

But, in fact, it only lasted a few months. In a move that shocked the U.N., the American Ambassador, Henry J. Sontag, submitted U.N. Resolution 14982.c., stating "that while South America was allowed to continue to be infested and untouched, the 'living' world would be in constant danger".

An obvious fact, but the statement brought everyone back on point. The Resolution proposed that the United States be given sovereignty over South America.

In his impassioned speech, Sontag said, "This danger lays at the very feet of our nation. America is the most threatened, and the bastion between the dark tide of walking dead and the rest of the world. If we fall, then Canada and Alaska will follow, adding their numbers growing by millions. Then they will cross the Baring Sea into northern Europe, and, ladies and gentlemen, they *will* cross. Let's stop our posturing, and enjoy a refreshing moment of honesty. Each member here knows how dire their own country's needs are. How each has suffered. I ask you, if any one of you believes their country can sustain another blow, another swarm of seething undead... then let them raise their hand. If not, then pass this resolution, and I promise you, you are guaranteeing that you will never see another of your country's innocent children mutilated in the teeth of this walking evil."

Although the other countries initially objected, calling it a bald-face land grab, they soon realized that this would save them trillions in financial aid, and placate the growing unrest that was threatening some governments, whose grip on control was balancing on the head of a pin. In short, South America was a ticking time bomb, and the United States had just volunteered to take it home. United Nations Resolution 14982.c. was unanimously signed on August 3rd, 2028. South America was annexed to the United States. Many in the Congress and Senate considered this to be political genius, while others said it was the worst mistake ever made.

The U.N. Resolution had been conceived, written, and fast-tracked to the President's desk in under a week. The immediate Cabinet members were given a two hour briefing that left no room to get into the details, let alone be reviewed by the advisers to the Cabinet members, who would have sent up more red flags than a Moscow parade.

The gratification that came with the political victory of winning over South America was short lived. The reality of what the politicians had just laid at the feet of the American people set in quickly.

In essence, the politicians had just bought, sight unseen, a 6.8 million square mile fixer-upper, containing three active, but abandoned nuclear reactors, countless smaller power plants, oil refineries and natural gas pumping stations, all of which represented a cluster of potential ticking time bombs that could go off without warning. And, just to make things interesting, the entire area was infested by an unknown number of inhabitants waiting to eat you alive.

It was decided that traditional military resources would be used for the general eradication of the undead. Using a proven tactic from history, an area would be cleared, or stabilized, and then they'd create a forward operating base (FOB), much like forts of the old west. Using this strategy, the plan was to leapfrog ever further into the country, creating FOBs along the way. Once resources were established at an FOB, such as water and power, they would then populate the bases with civilians, create micro-economies and the FOB would expand, while transitioning from a military base to a secured civilian town.

The AVEF

With many countries in disarray, and their own military defense capabilities badly crippled, the more suspicious members of the U.N. argued that the rapid increase of American military forces may be building up an invasion force.

Alliances were uncertain. Several foreign powers were fighting for their survival against coups and civil wars; you never knew who was in charge from one day to the next. The anonymous nuclear strike from the year before hadn't been forgotten, and it was decided it would be wiser to not provoke further doubts, so the United States agreed to embed U.N. inspectors to observe and report on troop movements.

No country is comfortable with complete transparency, and the U.S. was no exception; it was felt that giving the rest of the world troop movements and locations could be used against them.

There needed to be a way to augment the military, but bypass U.N. Oversight.

With this in mind, the AVEF was created. The All Volunteer Expeditionary Force (AVEF) would be out of sight of the U.N. by establishing it within the existing 'non-combatant' military unit of

Mortuary Affairs. The AVEF would keep its name, but throughout the entire military they would be known as the Grave Diggers.

Primarily manned by volunteers, the men and women were put through FEWS; Fast Emerson in Weapons and Survival. Since they would not be facing an enemy that utilized tactics or any form of combined assault profiles, the need for training beyond the use of a weapon and triage medical aid was considered unneeded. In addition, it was deemed that the needs of the AVEF wouldn't require newer or top of the line weaponry used by other ground units. After all, it's not like they need to defeat body armor. So instead, they were supplied with surplus, which wasn't much of a problem, except that equipment like radios and more technically complex gear was prone to failure.

1

PATROL

Eight figures moved with tense caution through the gloom of the jungle. The thick canopy of trees towered eighty feet above them, trapping air and wetness like a lid on a simmering pot, creating a thick, fermented mist below. Where sunlight could find its way through the canopy, it looked like misty pillars of gold.

The uninitiated were exhausted after five miles, just from the effort of breathing. Sweating did nothing to cool them down, because the high humidity kept sweat from evaporating; dehydration could kill just as quickly as the scorpions, snakes, and spiders. The jungle was thick with the sounds of animals; monkeys, birds, frogs, bugs, all communicating over each other, making the rainforest anything but peaceful, and easily masking the sounds of approaching threats.

The eight figures moved in single file and stopped when the one in the lead brought up a clinched fist. The leader crouched, as the other seven did their best to move quietly into the nearest shadows.

Sergeant Lori Wesson knelt alone. Her pale green eyes scanned the surroundings. Almost everything looked normal. Almost.

The radio in her ear gave a short hiss. "What is it, Sergeant?"

Her mike boom was nearly close enough to touch her lips, making her whispered voice easy to hear. "One of our trip wires has been set off. I'm checking it out."

By confirmation, her radio hissed again. "Okay. Squad, keep your eyes open. Wesson will recon."

Wesson went forward a short distance, studying her surroundings, then stopped. With a final scan of the area, she bent down to examine the ground.

"Staff Sergeant," whispered Wesson. "I got tracks."

With a quiet grunt, Staff Sergeant Jack Tate shrugged off his combat pack, working his shoulders to ease the pain where the straps bit into his shoulders. Leaving the concealing shadows, he quietly joined Wesson.

Tate took off his worn boonie cap as he knelt next to Wesson, and examined the tracks she had found.

The camouflage of his Army Combat Uniform was faded and sweat-stained, but did the job of helping him blend into the surroundings.

He opened his canteen and dribbled some water onto his boonie cap to cool his head, even though the relief was only temporary.

He saw that the carpet of fallen leaves had been disturbed in a wide path that lead into the trees ahead. Tracks were expected, but still an unwelcome wrinkle.

"What do you think? How long since they were here?"

"A day, maybe two," said Wesson. She scraped away some dirt, exposing damp soil below. "This top soil has dried and it hasn't rained here for a few days." She pointed at a busy tail of fire ants. "You can see where these ants had to rebuild their path after it was disturbed." She moved up a few feet, then came back. "I can't give an exact number, but judging by the tracks there's more than five. Less than fifteen."

Sighing, Tate ran his fingers through his short, ash-blond hair and keyed up his mike.

"Team," he said, as he put on his cap and combat pack, "line up on me. We got signs of contact. Ten Victor Mikes, plus or minus."

The remaining six members gathered behind Tate.

The radioman looked around anxiously. All of his gear had that 'just out of the box' look, while the rest of the team's were worn and faded.

He tapped the soldier in front of him, who looked over his shoulder, slightly annoyed. "What?"

"What's a Victor Mike?" asked the radioman.

The soldier frowned at him with disapproval, but said nothing.

"It's my first patrol," said the radioman, apologetically.

The soldier sighed in disgust. "Victor Mike. Victus mortuus. Latin for 'living and dead', stupid. Don't they teach you nothing at boot camp?"

"You don't call them Zombies?" asked the radioman.

"Don't be such a noob," grumbled the soldier. "Nobody says that anymore. Victor Mike, or Vix for short."

"Hey, quiet back there," crackled Tate's voice over the radio.

The soldier looked at the radioman like he was dirt. "Keep your hole shut, noob," said the soldier, and turned his back on him.

Wesson took up the point position and waved the patrol forward into the shadows.

After going a few miles further the patrol came to a break in the jungle that opened up to a wide, flat landscape, dotted with small clusters of trees and tall brown grass. Half a mile ahead was a small village.

Tate signaled the team to spread out and stay hidden in the tree line. Taking out his compact binoculars, he scanned the village.

Wesson did the same.

Tate swept his glasses to a cargo container a few hundred yards away from the village. The sun was on the opposite side of the container, casting a shadow on Tate's side, but he could still make out it was painted with a camo pattern, and had a radio antenna on top of it.

Heat waves rippled his view of the landscape, but he couldn't detect any other movement.

Tate took down his binoculars and wiped the sweat off his face.

He caught Wesson looking at him expectantly. "All right, let's see if anyone's home." Tate keyed his mike. "Radio."

Down the line, the radio operator was staring, wide eyed, at the village. This was his first patrol, and it showed from his new gear to the white-knuckled death grip on his M203 grenade launcher.

When he didn't respond to Tate's call for the radio, the solider next to the new kid gave him a light slap on the back of the head.

"Hey, dipstick, the staff sergeant just called you."

The kid nodded and wiped the sweat from his face, then looked up and down the line, unsure where to go.

Sighing, the soldier pointed in Tate's direction. "No noise," he said, as the rookie moved past him.

Crouching low, the kid made his way to Tate, who wore an expression of tired impatience. He could see the new guy was nervous, and Tate softened his expression.

"What's your name, Private?"

"Egg Beater," blurted the private, then catching his mistake he tried again. "Uh, I mean that's my call sign, from boot camp."

Tate was still waiting, and the private wished he could disappear. "Paul. I mean Keeble, Staff Sergeant," he said. "Private Keeble."

Tate looked at him firmly, but without blame. "Private Keeble, look at this team and tell me what you see."

Keeble glanced at the squad members quickly, wanting to avoid eye contact. "Soldiers, Staff Sergeant?"

Tate chose to ignore Keeble's reply was more a question than an answer. "That's right, Private. Soldiers who got the same training you did. They followed that training and it hasn't failed them. Follow your training, and it won't fail you."

"Yes, Staff Sergeant," said Keeble, his anxiety coming down several notches.

"Good," said Tate. "Now, get me that observation post on the radio, and let's see what we're dealing with."

Keeble pulled out a list of frequencies related to their patrol area, and punched in the numbers. "OP Charlie, how copy, over?" He waited a few seconds for a reply, but got nothing. He tried again with the same results.

Wesson leaned in close to Tate. "That was nice of you, to take time with Keeble."

Tate scanned the area surrounding the observation post for a long time.

"Hoo-ah, Sergeant. As long as he believes it, maybe he'll live a little longer." He wiped the sweat off his neck and looked out at the observation post thoughtfully.

Wesson rolled her eyes and put away her binoculars. "The OP's not responding. I'm going to check it out." She gave Tate a disapproving look and keyed up her mike. "Yeler, you're with me."

"Hang on, Sergeant, I'll do it. Besides," said Tate, patting the spread of his stomach, "I need the exercise. Sergeant Wesson, you and the rest of the team will provide cover. Private Keeble, keep trying to raise the OP. If we run into any Vix use your grenade launcher and drop smoke rounds. That'll confuse them and buy us time to get out of there, got it?"

"Yes, copy, Staff Sergeant," said Keeble.

Wesson followed Tate as he unbuckled his pack and propped it against a tree. "I think I should go, Staff Sergeant."

Tate did a quick check of his battered M4 rifle, then slung it over his shoulder. "How would it look on my patrol report if my sergeant did all the work? The captain would accuse me of being, how did you put it, apathetic and disinterested?"

"You weren't supposed to see that report," said Wesson.

"I won't lie," said Tate. "That part about apathetic stung. I would have gone with cynical. Reports aren't your style. Let me guess, the captain was behind it, right?"

"He's reached his limit with you. It can't be a surprise. You're a staff sergeant, but you don't lead, you don't invest in your men. No disrespect, but I don't know why you're even here."

"This is quite a rare moment of candor for you, Sergeant Wesson," grinned Tate. Then he turned serious. "My situation's complicated. I'm here because... this is all I know." He looked like he was going to say more, but changed his mind and walked back to the edge of the tree line.

A moment later, Tate and Yeler left the trees into the tall grass. Tate turned the volume on his radio off and motioned to Yeler to do the same. Moving quietly, they stayed low with their heads just above the grass, both of them scanning for any danger.

The crunch of the dry grass made Tate wince, but even a ninja would have made noise here. He kept glancing at the cargo container for signs of movement, but nothing stirred, only the constant hum and clicks of insects.

In reality, the cargo container was a mobile observation post, made of honeycomb plastic walls to act as a sound buffer, so noise inside couldn't be heard from outside. It was light enough to be carried by a Black Hawk helicopter, and put down just about anywhere. Once in position, it could be covered in brush, or a camo net. Self-contained to house two soldiers whose assignment was to monitor and report, Tate's squad was there because the OP had missed their last three check-ins.

Tate and Yeler reached the near side of the OP, and took a moment in the shade. Tate thought he could hear the hiss of a radio and both men confirmed it wasn't theirs.

Each side of the OP had a non-reflective tinted window, making it impossible to see in from the outside.

They moved around to the access doors in the back, but they were locked.

"This is Tate," he said into his mike. "It's locked up tight and there's no sign of..."

Suddenly Tate and Yeler heard a crackle of static, and Private Keeble's voice.

"OP Charlie, please respond, over."

Puzzled, Tate and Yeler looked at each other, wondering where that just came from. It hadn't come over their radios.

"Radio silence," whispered Tate into his mike.

Back at the tree line, Wesson keyed her mike twice to acknowledge the message. Through her binoculars, Wesson could read the body language of the two men. Both of them had just cranked up their alertness.

The other squad members strained to see what was happening across the field.

"That was the OP radio," said Yeler, quietly. "We shouldn't have heard that through these soundproof walls, right?"

Tate nodded in agreement. "I think it came from the other side. Come on."

Everything about this was wrong, and Tate didn't like any of it.

He didn't like the OP missing their check-in. He didn't like recon missions, because you never knew what dangers waited for you. He didn't like being out in the open with no cover for hundreds of yards. And he didn't like the apprehension that was crawling up his spine.

They moved around to the sunny side of the OP, and stopped cold. Both of them gripped their weapons and scanned the surrounding grass with renewed unease.

The side of the OP had been ripped open, leaving a gaping hole. Chunks and shards of the honeycombed wall laid scattered on the flattened grass in front of the nearly man-sized hole; now they knew why they could hear the radio inside.

"See that?" asked Tate, as he motioned to several bullet holes in the wrecked wall. "No bullet casings out here."

"Meaning all the shots were fired from inside the OP," said Yeler. "No signs of any Vix."

Tate brought up his rifle and softly pushed the safety off with his thumb. It was old, but reliable.

Yeler slung his SCAR 17S over his shoulder and drew his Glock.

With Tate watching the area around them, Yeler tried to see inside the OP. The stark pillar of light punching through the hole of the OP restricted Yeler's eyes from adjusting to the shadows deeper inside.

He moved his hat to shield the sun from his eyes, while pointing his pistol in the same direction he was looking.

"Can't see much," he said, leaning further through the hole into the OP. Grumbling in annoyance, he fumbled for his flashlight.

"Tick tock," said Tate, urging Yeler to speed up.

Yeler straightened up, offering his flashlight to Tate with a grin. "Hey, if you think you got better eyes for this, I'm more than happy to..."

Suddenly, a rotted hand flashed out of the darkened OP, grabbing Yeler by the face. The fingers punched through the flesh of his cheek and eye socket, and ripped away half of his face.

Yeler's scream died to a gurgle, as a gush of blood clogged his throat.

Time slowed to a crawl as Tate's mind tried to comprehend the horror in front of him.

Yeler staggered back, holding what was left of his face.

Tate could see each drop of blood in minute detail as it spurted between Yeler's fingers. With his other hand, Yeler was pulling the trigger of his pistol. Each flash of the gun looked like a slow bloom of fire, yet there was no sound.

Into this nightmare, something horrific appeared from the hole in the OP. Ripped flesh hung in ragged ribbons from its face. One shriveled eye swung from the socket.

In slow motion, it shoved the handful of Yeler's shattered face into its mouth and turned its gaze to Tate. Its remaining eye glowed with lustful menace, as it started to climb out of the hole.

The air was ripped as one of Yeler's shots narrowly missed Tate's head, and snapped him out of his trance; what had happened in seconds seemed like hours.

Instinct took over, and Tate yanked a grenade from his combat vest, pulled the pin and dropped it.

Without looking back, he ran around the other side of the OP and bolted for the tree line and his squad.

"Contact, contact! Single Vic," Tate yelled into his mike.

His voice electrified the squad.

They brought up their guns and panned the field, ready to annihilate any sign of movement.

A flash of light and crack of explosion rocked the OP, as the grenade went off.

Tate was half way across the field when a Vix rose up in the grass; then another, and another.

Four corpses turned towards Tate and charged. Two were badly decayed and very slow, but the other two were lethally fast.

Tate was putting everything he had into running flat-out, and didn't look around to see how many there were; the only important thing was not slowing down, but twenty extra pounds and being out of shape was already affecting him. Speed and his squad were the only things keeping him alive.

In the tree line, the squad members began firing. The two slower corpses were easy targets and went down quickly, but they weren't the problem since the staff sergeant was easily outdistancing them. The other dead were madly sprinting towards Tate from his left, and closing.

"Smoke," yelled Tate. "Smoke!" It felt like an eternity until he heard the distant *thunk* sound of Private Keeble's grenade launcher.

Any second there'd be a plume of smoke he could run into and make his escape.

An instant later, the ground ahead of him exploded in a fountain of dirt and shrapnel. In his panic, Keeble hadn't switched a grenade shell for a smoke round, and just fired it off. Hot metal peppered Tate's face and chest like burning needles, but he couldn't dare slow down.

He heard a crack from a rifle, and saw from the corner of his eye a chunk blown off of one of the Vix, spinning it around. It disappeared into the grass.

An instant later it was back up, and racing after Tate, bone and goo flapping from a gaping wound where its arm used to be.

Tate's breath was ragged and his legs were starting to feel like they were filled with sand. Blood ran down his face, blurring his left eye as he bent his will to dig deep and push himself to keep pumping his legs.

The squad was shooting the instant they had a target, but the Vix were fast and their movements erratic. The best they could do was pour on the firepower and hope they hit something. Among the squad, there was one soldier who hadn't fired a shot.

Kasey Ota looked down the scope of his beloved Dragunov SVD, breathing slowly in and out. Through the scope, he could see the strain carved into Tate's face, but he didn't care.

Ota moved the crosshairs and found the Vic nearing Tate. Through the lens he watched as something yellow dribbled from the Vix's mouth, and its hands clawed at the air as it tried to reach Tate, but Ota didn't care.

All he cared about was his breathing. He focused on the sound of the air as it flowed through his nostrils and out of his mouth. The numbing roar of gunfire around him didn't exist.

His mind was void of right or wrong, time or need. He drifted his sights slightly ahead of the dashing corpse and counted his breathing.

Tate could feel his body failing him. He wasn't the young man he used to be, and the end of his energy was about to give out as abruptly as the tug of a hangman's rope.

Gunfire from the tree line was tapering off, which told him the Vix were so close now that many of his team were afraid of hitting him.

He reached for his pistol. In the next second, he'd either use it on the Vix or himself.

Suddenly his shoulder was yanked, as the hissing corpse latched onto his web gear.

The Vix's mouth gaped open as it pulled itself to Tate.

He raised his pistol, but fate was making the gun feel too heavy; too slow. He'd be dead before he ever pulled the trigger. He could hear the thing's teeth snapping next to his ear with perfect clarity, and knew it was over.

Tate flinched as something slapped air right next to his face, with a stinging buzz.

The entire top of the Vix's head vanished in a fine mist, and it crumpled to the ground.

Before Tate could react to the second corpse, it was blown off its feet, spraying skull fragments behind it.

Ota pulled back the bolt of his rifle, spinning the spent cartridge into the air, aware of the looks of amazement from the rest of his team.

A moment later, Tate staggered into the tree line, rejoining his team. His legs trembled as he bent over, gasping for air.

Wesson handed him a canteen, which he poured over his head, washing off dust, blood, and ooze. Drenched in sweat and water, he motioned for the radioman.

Riddled with guilt, Keeble began to explain. "I'm sorry, Staff Sergeant. The grenade... I panicked..."

With a surprising resource of energy, Tate slammed Keeble across the jaw with a sledgehammer blow.

The Private rag-dolled to the ground, unconscious.

"Keep him out of my sight," gasped Tate, "for the rest of the patrol... or I'll kill him... where he stands."

Ota walked past the inert private with mild curiosity, and handed Tate his backpack. "Can we go home now, Staff Sergeant?"

2

CIUDAD DE ROSE

Jack Tate looked out at the passing neon lights of the city from the back seat of a taxi. Every time it went around a corner, the thing leaned like a ship riding a high wave. The springs squeaked like tortured steel, but at least it was clean and the driver didn't play his music loud. It seemed to Tate that every time he came into town something had changed, but he figured that was what life was like in the frontier towns of the old west, and in many ways, Ciudad de Rosa was no different.

Located in the narrow straights that connected North and South America, Ciudad de Rosa started as a refugee camp, which grew into a city. Named after the patron saint of South America, Saint Rose of Lima, the city was cradled between two massive mountain ranges that followed either coast. Between it and the untamed, malignant continent of undead was Fort Hickok, the U.S. Army installation, and Tates home, used as a staging area for the newly formed branch for dealing with clearing out South America.

Originally, Ciudad de Rosa had three thousand people, until it exploded with the migration of refugees. That also brought opportunity for businesses big, small, and illegal. The black market used to thrive with the transportation of drugs coming out of the country, and when that stopped, it adapted to other financial trades.

Now, Ciudad de Rosa was a stark contradiction of itself. Extravagant homes occupied hundreds of acres of land, like mini fiefdoms, making Beverly Hills look like a slum.

Refugees lived in a sprawling camp of tents, huts and anything they could hold together to give them a roof and walls to keep the snakes, fire ants and scorpions out.

A few factories had set up in the hopes of capitalizing on the cheap labor, until they discovered the cost of putting peasant farmers in a factory setting. In the end, many companies had to set up training courses.

Overall, the city was well behaved. Criminals on both ends of the financial scale knew things ran smoother when everyone got along. The realists in the police department understood what they could and couldn't do; there were places in Ciudad de Rosa where the law never went. Besides, by the time they showed up, the problem had already been sorted out, or the only ones to interview were dead. So, the city thrummed along at an easy pace, with little upheaval.

Jack Tate had left the army base after working up his action report, and Private Keeble's transfer forms.

The captain had torn into him, threatening that he'd jump past an Article 15 and go for a court martial. It was white noise to Tate; his mind was far away from the squawks of his CO.

He stood at attention and waited for the yelling to stop, then left without a word.

It was his time now, and he was tired of seeing anything in camo. He knew a club in part of the city that was perfectly situated beneath trendy and above seedy.

The Blue Orchid could have been in the nicer areas of town if the owner could afford it, but the bouncers kept the dirt out, so it was okay with Tate.

The taxi pulled up outside the club, and Tate got out. He noticed a small tremor in his hand as he paid the driver. He was having trouble turning his back on today's mission.

As the taxi pulled away, Tate took a moment to fill his lungs with the evening air.

A bouncer standing at the entrance passively watched him.

The owner, Teddy Moon, didn't like the expression 'bouncer', and called them doormen, believing it gave the place some class. He was also a big fan of the 1940s noir movies, and it showed from the club's decor to the music; if you didn't like Glenn Miller or Harry James, this was the wrong place for you.

The doorman looked like a stack of boulders and just as solid. Tate couldn't tell if his face was naturally flat, or the result of stopping a lot of punches. If it was the latter, he was sure that face had left a trail of broken hands behind it. He was typical of the 'doorman' Teddy hired. It was impossible to get drunk enough to believe you could take on one of these guys, and yet all of them were civil and polite. He moved aside as Tate approached.

"Evening, Mr Jack."

"Evening, Rocko," said Tate. He didn't believe that was his real name, but Teddy Moon had a thing for nicknames, and if you stood still long enough, Teddy would put one on you.

Rocko was as good a name as anyone could have come up with, and in this case, it was a good fit.

"Looks crowded tonight."

"That's how the boss likes it. But there's always room for you, Mr Jack. Enjoy yourself." Rocko opened the door, and Tate stepped inside.

Tate walked in, greeted by the jukebox playing That Old Black Magic. The lighting was easy on the eyes; not too dark, but lit well enough to see around the place.

The club was done up as close to looking like some place Bogart would get a drink at. Leather, brass and wood made up most of the décor, although on closer inspection everything had a worn look to it; some might think it was aged and shabby, but to Tate it just felt lived in.

He looked around for an open seat at the bar; sitting alone at a booth made him feel alone and self-conscious.

"Jaaaaack," someone called across the room.

Teddy Moon crossed the club floor to Tate, with a large smile and friendly handshake.

"It's a pleasure to see you, old man," said Teddy warmly. "Welcome back to the Blue Orchid."

"Thanks, Teddy," said Tate. "Nice to be back."

"Teddy? Don't be so formal," said Teddy. "All my friends call me Commodore." Tate had no idea how or why Teddy had come up with that nickname, but it did no good to ask.

He was well groomed, and always in fashion should the 1940s ever come back. Tonight, he was wearing a simple but well-tailored, double-breasted jacket, with a white dress shirt and tie. His cologne was a warm mix of tobacco, citrus and leather, and he never went anywhere without it.

Tate didn't go out of his way to make friends, or be chummy, but Teddy had that kind of personality that you couldn't help but like.

"Let's see. You'll be wanting a place at the bar, right?" asked Teddy, without really asking. He glanced at the bar and saw it was full.

Tate wasn't feeling picky, and would have settled for anyplace that wasn't the center of Teddy's attention.

"It's okay. I can sit anywhere."

But Teddy wasn't listening. He escorted Tate to the end of the bar, where a couple of girls were talking.

"Ladies," said Teddy. "Excuse me, but it's just come to my attention that these seats were the victim of someone's over indulgence, and I'll have to ask you to move to one of the booths while we clean them up."

The girls looked at Teddy, uncomprehending. Few people talked like Teddy, and it took awhile to get used to him, although he understood himself perfectly and therefore believed everyone else did, too.

The girls continued to stare at Teddy as they waited for him to say something they understood.

"A guy threw up on your seats," he said impatiently.

The girls leapt off the seats like they'd just been stabbed by a pin, craning their heads around, looking for stains on the rear of their tight dresses.

"Yes, it's horrible," said Teddy, as he took each of them by an arm, leading them over to an empty booth and sitting them down. "I'll have your drinks brought over to you."

"We left our purses at the bar," objected one of the girls.

"I'll have them sent over," said Teddy.

"What about our bill?" asked the other girl.

"I'll have that brought over, too," said Teddy, leaving them gaping at his back.

Tate couldn't help but smirk as Teddy came over and sat him at the bar, leaving an empty seat between Tate and the other patrons.

"Bertie," said Teddy, catching the bartender's attention. "Take care of my friend here."

Then to Tate, "I heard things got dicey on your outing today. You're at the Blue Orchid now, so put your feet up and take it easy."

Tate was troubled, but not surprised that Teddy knew about the patrol; it wasn't difficult for him to believe that Teddy's enterprises reached beyond running a nightclub.

"I don't suppose you'd tell me how you always know so much?"

Teddy appraised Tate with a smile that held more meaning than he was willing to explain.

"The Blue Orchid caters to those who pay in currency other than money, and speaking of money, keep your wallet in your pocket tonight. It's on the house. If you need anything else, just give me the high sign."

Before Tate could ask what the 'high sign' was, Teddy was gone.

Bertie looked at Tate, patiently waiting for his order. "I'd like a bourbon."

The bartender gave him a slight nod and reached under the counter for a bottle. He put a tumbler in front of Tate and filled the bottom of it.

The aroma of alcohol and oak coming from his glass filled his senses, and he could feel himself beginning to relax.

Bertie left him to take care of others along the bar, which was fine with Tate; it was just him and a glass of smooth bourbon.

He held the tumbler up to his nose, closing his eyes as he inhaled. He let his mind drift around the sounds of the bar, while he settled against the bar.

Suddenly, his peace was shattered with blood and screaming. Images of Yeler's shattered face filled his mind. Horror gripped at

Tate, and his eyes shot open, finding only a dimly lit club filled with people. The memory faded, leaving his trembling hand holding the tumbler.

Startled and angry, Tate knocked back his drink in one swallow. He stopped himself from banging the tumbler down on the bar-top, and struggled to get his emotions back under control.

The bartender appeared and poured his glass again.

Tate held up his hand, before the bartender walked off.

"Hang on, Bertie. You're going to be pouring a few more of those in a minute." Tate lifted his glass, about to empty it in one swig, when a hand landed heavily on his shoulder.

"You need a good cigar with bourbon," said a friendly voice. "Anything less is a crime."

Recognizing the voice, Tate stood up and saluted. "Good evening, Colonel Hewett."

"Sit down, Jack," smiled Hewett. "I'll have one of those," he said to the bartender, pointing to Tate's drink.

The colonel sat in the stool next to Tate and reached into his jacket, taking out a small cigar case. He slid two cigars from the case and offered one to Tate.

"No, thank you, sir," said Tate.

"Let's leave the 'sir' back at the base," said Hewett. Replacing one of the cigars, he put the case back in his jacket pocket.

The bartender produced a cigar cutter and lighter for Hewett, who took them with a nod.

"I like this place. I can see why you come here." He snipped the end off the cigar, and put it in his mouth. He started the lighter and held the flame to the end of the cigar, while he puffed on it a couple of times until the end briefly glowed a dark orange.

Tate watched the colonel go through the ritual. He'd met Earl Hewett a year earlier, when he first joined the A.V.E.F., and they had immediately clicked. There's a connection soldiers share who have been through the merciless forge of combat. They don't wear it on their sleeve. It's something in their presence, a vibe that other soldiers of shared experiences recognize instinctually, and in spite of his lax demeanor, the colonel saw it in Tate.

Tate had a mixed opinion of officers, but appreciated that the colonel cared about those under his command. When he was on base, the colonel was often seen away from his desk, talking to his junior officers, watching the units going through their training, combat shooting practice, etc.

What had Tate curious was that he and Hewett didn't socialize on or off the base. Following the normal chain of command, Tate reported through his captain. He'd bet good money the colonel wasn't here by coincidence, and sooner or later he'd get around to it; as it was, Tate didn't have to wait long.

"You know, Jack, if you stay in the Army long enough, you either become a very good politician, or a very good soldier. If you're not good at either, you end up dead either way. I think you're a good soldier."

"No disrespect, sir, but I know a lot of people that would disagree with you," said Tate.

"You know what they say about opinions and assholes, Jack. It's true most good soldiers get weary of the death," said Hewett. "It wears them down. When their tour's up, they retire and go home, which is why the Army is top heavy with politicians."

Hewett took a sip of bourbon, followed by a long draw on his cigar. He blew out the smoke slowly and took a sip of his bourbon. "I'm wondering why you haven't gone home."

Tate was beginning to dislike where this was going. His past was a topic he avoided talking about, but when put on the spot he'd lie. Lying made him uncomfortable. Not that he couldn't; on the contrary, he could lie easily and be convincing, but lies left behind tracks that a clever person might discover. He didn't have to worry about that this time.

"For example, I heard about a guy, Jack Tiller, that served with the 471st until a couple of years ago," said Hewett. "That's one of those hush-hush Delta, special mission units. They get the messy jobs nobody wants to do, or admit doing. They keep to themselves mostly. Not a lot of guys have their unit tattoo. Easy to spot, though." The colonel stopped and eyed Tate expectantly for a reaction, but Tate stared, stone faced, at his glass.

"So, this guy, Jack Tiller, one day he just ups and vanishes into thin air. Those spec-op guys are a tight-lipped family, and they wouldn't say anything else, but I did hear some chatter that something bad happened at home."

Tate only nodded, but said nothing as the colonel took his time getting to the point. Tate wasn't in a hurry either, and waited to see how many gaps the colonel would fill in.

"Must have been pretty bad for this guy, Tiller, to quit an entire life just like that."

"Must have," Tate said, as he stared into his glass.

"Part of my brigade is the Mortuary Affairs, where they slipped in the All Volunteer Expeditionary Force. Those AVEFs aren't even real soldiers, not that the Army would complain. They need all the bodies they can to make a dent clearing out those rotting meat sticks. They'll take anyone who walks in the door, so it's not hard to imagine how low the bar's set on performance. Hell, if they can button their own shirt we're satisfied, so when your name kept showing up on action reports I got curious. Where the life expectancy in that unit is a few months, you're not only alive and kicking, but demonstrating advanced squad tactics. The kind of tactics someone with special training would have."

Tate knew he'd been found out, but was too annoyed and stubborn to admit it.

"Knock it off, Jack. I don't have any more time for this crap." He was tired of this game, and had used up what patience he had for innuendos. "Show it to me," he said, bumping Tate in the shoulder with his knuckles.

The colonel knew too much for Tate to claim ignorance. With a sigh, he pushed up his right sleeve, exposing a tattoo. It had two snakes intertwined up the handle of a double bladed executioners axe. It was framed with a shield and three words surrounding the axe, 'Iudex Iudices Carnificem'.

"Well, isn't that a thing," said the colonel in mock surprise. "My Latin's rusty. Iudex, Iudices, Carnificem. Judge, jury and executioner. Did I get that right?"

"What else do you know, or want to know?" sighed Tate.

Hewett took another pull on his cigar. Now that he was confident he had the right man, the hard part was out of the way.

"I know you were one of the best operators the 471st had. I know you have a box full of medals and ribbons, probably stuffed away somewhere. I know you pulled some hellacious high-risk missions, deep infiltration and high value terminations. I could go on, but I think I'm hitting inside the ten ring."

"I wouldn't know about any of that, Colonel."

Hewett chuckled and sipped his bourbon. "I'm sure you wouldn't. What I don't get is why a highly skilled operator would go off the reservation, and a year later sign up in a loser detail, scrubbing the worlds toilet."

Tate's glass stopped halfway to his mouth, and he put it down on the bar hard, rattling the ice cubes. "With all respect, sir, where is this going?"

"Come on, Jack, you snake eaters all have it in you. You guys can't resist testing yourselves, pushing yourself to the next level. Honing your skills."

Tate didn't say anything, but rolled his sleeve back down, covering his tattoo.

"Since you've been in Mortuary Affairs you've been drag-assing your way from one commander to another. The word is you're on your last leg. Your captain's going to file a court martial and probably get it. Anyone else and I'd say they deserve it, but I don't think that's you. You act like you hate the Army, but you always seem to do just enough to keep from getting kicked out, until now, and I think that was a mistake. That wasn't part of your plan. If you wanted out, you would have been gone a long time ago."

Tate emptied the last of his drink, wishing the bourbon would hurry up and blur the world out of existence. "Well, if that was true, and I'm not saying it is... or isn't, none of that matters, now. I don't think the captain'll have much trouble getting his court martial, and I'll be gone."

"Which brings me to answering your unspoken question, of why I'm here. Ever since we got South America, the prevailing strategy has been to systematically work our way across the country, wiping out the Vix as we go. It's a simple plan. Easy to execute, easy to understand, and wrong. Our country is in trouble. I don't have to tell you the devastation we've suffered because of the outbreak. Our infrastructure is broken and some of us have done the math. The current plan is too little, too late.

"Jack, the country will collapse if we don't do something fast. South America has silver, copper and gold mines, oil fields and natural gas that we desperately need. Those resources would go a long way to getting our country on her feet again. But the government refuses to see the danger. They're so afraid to admit their plan isn't working, that they reject anyone who disagrees with them, discrediting in public as alarmist. There are some who aren't willing to sit back and watch the government drive the country into an early grave. They've come together from branches of military, corporations, and even a few in the government. The objective is to scout out the most accessible resources, ones we can tap into and bring online with the least amount of expended assets, then the government will have no choice but to change its direction."

"And you want to form a covert unit inside the AVEF, right?" said Tate.

"Exactly. They're so insignificant on everyone's radar, it's the perfect place to operate from."

Tate swirled the ice cubes in his glass, watching the play of light winking off them. "Why are you telling me about this? Whatever you think you know about my past, I'm not that guy. The most exercise I get is convincing myself to get out of bed in the morning."

He didn't show it, but the prospect of running operations again was making his heartbeat quicken. He knew the colonel was trying to read him. Tate kept an attitude of bored interest; he wasn't going to give the colonel any emotional leverage.

"I'm not looking for supermen, but I do need a guy with experience under his belt. You'd be tasked with creating a small unit," said the colonel, "which would conduct specialized missions to insert and recon suspected high value targets."

Hewett lightly rapped his cigar on the edge of the ashtray, knocking off the ash and giving Tate time to digest what he'd heard.

"You report back, and we send in assets to collect the resources. That simple." Hewett took a sip of his drink, saving the best part of his offer for last. "I'll authorize your request for a limited number of promotions within your unit, and you'd be promoted to sergeant major, as befitting your responsibility."

Tate couldn't hide his expression of surprise. "That's three grades. Nobody's going to sign off on that, and even if they did, that's going to attract a lot of attention to your *secret* unit."

Hewett tapped the rank insignia on the shoulder of his uniform. "That bird means I do the worrying. All you need to do is sign on. Besides, wasn't that your rank in the 471st? You earned it, you wear it."

Hewett paused, giving Tate time to consider his offer. He casually looked around the room for a few moments, buying himself some time. The next part of the conversation could get rocky, but this was too important and he wasn't going to shy away from it.

"It'll be your unit. Your people," said the colonel. "The thing is, Jack, a man of your experience is hard to come by, and would be a great benefit to me, but I have to know you're squared away." Hewett looked straight at him, studying Tate's every expression.

"I need to know you aren't going to bail on me the first time you feel inconvenienced. You were a highly decorated, highly skilled soldier that walked away from friends and career without a word of explanation. Then, out of the blue you sign up in the crap shoveler unit that follows the elephant parade. I think you'd be a perfect fit for my unit, but I have to know I can rely on you. I have to know your men can rely on you. I can't have you quitting on me because of some bullshit baggage."

A visible coolness came over Tate, but Hewett saw beyond the mask to the anger Tate was barely controlling.

"I have never let my men down, or been accused of failing in my duties as a soldier," said Tate, through an expression of stone. "And, my *bullshit baggage*," the words were sticking in his throat, "was because while I was away on a mission, when I should have been home..." Tate forced himself to take a breath. He lifted his drink to his lips, but changed his mind and put the tumbler back down.

"My little girl, who I should have been protecting, was torn to pieces by a pack of Vix. So yes, I've never failed my men, but I failed my little girl. I failed my wife. Every time she looked at me, all she saw was the man responsible for her sorrow. The single most important thing I needed to do, and I failed."

"Well, hell," said the colonel. In a rare and unexpected expression of solace, Colonel Hewett put his hand on Tate's shoulder. "Anything I could say to lessen your grief would sound feeble, and dishonor the tremendous loss you've suffered," said Hewett, firmly squeezing Tate's shoulder. "I apologize for opening that wound."

The colonel got out of his seat and looked for a moment at Tate, who sat staring a thousand miles away.

Hewett was about to say something, but thought better of it and walked out the door.

Outside, the colonel's aid opened the door for him. Getting in the backseat, Hewett took out his cell phone and dialed a number.

Someone on the other end of the call picked up.

"Tate's a no-go. Yes, I told him what we're doing, but he's trustworthy. He's not a liability, so don't touch him."

Hewett listened while the aid patiently sat in the driver's seat, waiting for instructions from the colonel.

"Send me the file on our next candidate. I've got time..."

The colonel was interrupted by a rapping on the car window.

He lowered the smoked glass window to see Jack Tate, peering at him with disturbing intensity.

"Jack?"

Tate wordlessly stared at the colonel, who was feeling something close to fear creeping up on him.

"I'm in," said Tate, then walked away into the gloom of the night.

3

SHADOWS IN THE NIGHT

The barracks door slammed open, as a line of exhausted soldiers shuffled in from the dark of night. They were splattered with mud, and wet with sweat from having been out since the crack of dawn, and had thought of nothing but a shower and sacking out for the past two hours. Entering the barracks, they let out a collective groan.

The contents of their footlockers had been dumped all over the floor. Their bunks had been stripped of bedding, and the mattresses were skewed over the bunk frames. It looked like a tornado had ripped through the place, backed up and went through again. But this disaster was care of their drill instructor; a small lesson in digging deep into the gas tank when you think there's nothing left.

This was M Squad, or, as everyone called it, the Meat Squad. These were the new troops, fresh out of boot camp. It wasn't the traditional training regular soldiers got, where seasoned, tungsten hard drill instructors turned civilians into a soldier; M Squad had signed up for Mortuary Affairs because it was a non-combat unit, or so they thought.

The training they got in boot camp was just enough to teach recruits how to put on a uniform and dig a hole. All recruits arriving on base from boot camp were thrown into M Squad, and remained unassigned to their final units until they been given some real training.

One of the privates raced to his strewn belongings in near panic. Everyone else was too exhausted to notice or care, as the recruit searched through the mess while the rest of them worked to nearly put away their stuff.

Flinging open the lid of his footlocker, stenciled COOPER J., he tossed in his things until he spotted a toothbrush case, and snatched it up. He quickly glanced around to be sure nobody was looking his way, then opened the case.

He took out a folded up paper and stuffed it into his pocket, as relief washed over him.

By the time everyone had finished getting the barracks in order, it was 2AM. If anyone felt like crying, nobody would have blamed them, but they were too tired and dehydrated for the effort.

Before succumbing to fatigue, Private Cooper read through the instructions on the paper he'd retrieved from his toothbrush case. He knew it was important he got it right.

The last of the soldiers had collapsed into his bunk less than two hours ago, and the now orderly barracks was a hive of snoring.

Nobody heard the three figures enter their quarters. In the gloom, the figures were only visible when they were silhouetted against the dim moonlight through the windows.

There was no stealth in their actions. The scraping of feet could be heard as they dragged them across the floor. They didn't speak, but uttered low, wet guttural noises, and still no soldier stirred.

Klaxon alarms suddenly shattered the quiet of the night. Outside, spotlights flared to life, sweeping around the barracks as an urgent voice barked over the loudspeaker.

"Victor Mikes have breached security," blared the speaker. "They are in the camp! Vix are in the base!"

As the soldiers of Meat squad clawed their way out of sleep, one new recruit saw a figure looking down on him.

The outside spotlight momentarily lit the figure, searing its image into the recruits mind. Its hideously deformed face leered at him, its clothes, torn and black with dried blood. Something brown and shriveled spilled out of a gaping hole in its belly.

Another soldier caught a glimpse of a cadaverous woman, bent over a soldier's bunk, scooping bloody hunks to its face. The figure turned towards him and the spotlight passed, leaving only darkness and the sound of growling coming closer.

The horrified soldier tried to shout a warning, but his words became a scream as bony fingers closed around his face. He fumbled for the pistol near his bunk, madly pulling the trigger before the gun had even cleared the holster.

Any shred of sleep vanished in that instant. The barracks exploded in screams as gun fire strobe-lit the terror and panic consuming the soldiers. Except for one.

Before the klaxon alarm had sounded, before the undead creatures had gotten five feet into the barracks, Private Jared Cooper had quietly slipped off his bunk and slid under it.

He heard rather than saw the feet scraping by his bunk. Then the alarm had gone off, followed by the screaming. He waited until the sounds seemed to move away from him, and broke for the door.

Outside, a spotlight swept over two guards running by, and Cooper yelled for them. The guards stopped and pointed their rifles at him.

"I'm not bit," he said, as he ran to them. Before either guard could say a word, Cooper grabbed a grenade clipped to the guard's belt.

As the guard began to protest, Cooper yanked the rifle out of his arms and ran back to the barracks, with the guards chasing him.

As Cooper reached the barracks door, the screaming inside was near hysteria.

As the guards reached Cooper, he pulled the pin on the grenade.

"Back off," he yelled, holding the grenade over his head.

The guards turned and ran off.

Cracking open the door, Cooper threw the grenade inside, then dove for the ground. A moment later, there was a deafening crack and bright flash of light.

Cooper got to his feet, brought the stolen rifle to his shoulder and sprayed bullets into the barracks.

The rifle spat out the casing of the last bullet, and Cooper winced as the camp lights snapped on and the klaxons abruptly stopped.

The noise of the alarms was replaced by the shouts of several drill sergeants that seemed to magically appear from nowhere.

Unmoved, Cooper stood, gaze fixed on the door, hoping nothing would come through it.

"I said fall out," shouted a sergeant in Cooper's face, while taking the rifle out of his hands.

Open-mouthed, Cooper watched him stomp into the barracks, yelling, "Fall out, you stupid pukes!"

Dazed and disheveled, everyone in M squad lined up in front of their barracks, each looking at the other, trying to understand how they weren't dead.

Standing before them was a grim staff sergeant, staring at them with hard eyes.

"My name is Staff Sergeant Tate," he said, as he began walking along the line of ragged men. "You have just participated in a recreation of an event that occurred in your barracks when three Victor Mikes got onto this base. It is a special event we hold every time we get a new squad."

The door to their quarters slammed closed behind the row of men, and their eyes went wide as three ragged corpses walked by them and lined up next to the drill sergeants.

"It's evident the performance our actors played was convincing. Just like the actual event, only a few of you were attacked by our actors, and just like the actual event all of you died. How could this happen, you ask? Because each of you acted as an individual, instead of a unit. Your only interest was self-preservation, to live, regardless of what happened to the other guy. In short, you killed each other. Fortunately, all of your ammunition was replaced with paint ball munitions. If you look at your squad mates you can judge your effectiveness in protecting yourself, and them."

The recruits looked at each other, seeing they were pockmarked with blots of blue paint, with the exception of one; Private Cooper stood out from the other soldiers, completely untouched by blue paint.

"We hold this event so you'll feel welcomed here," continued Tate. "And to impress upon you that any slack behavior, lapse in judgment, or stupidity on your part could very well result in what you have experienced today."

Tate paused as he stood back and looked up and down the line of men. He looked at Cooper for the second time, and his expression hardened.

"Private," said Tate flatly to Cooper. "How is it that you are not dead?"

All the eyes of M squad fell on Cooper, who continued to look straight ahead. "Staff Sergeant," said Cooper. "Nobody wanted to bunk near the door because we were told in boot camp that's always the first person to die when a Victor Mike enters a barracks of sleeping soldiers. I got the short straw and had to take that bunk."

"And yet you are not dead, Private," said Tate.

"No, Staff Sergeant," said Cooper formally. "I tied a shoelace from the door handle to my finger. When the door opened, it woke me up. When I realized what had entered the barracks, I knew it was a no-win situation."

"Explain your meaning by saying 'no-win'," said Tate.

"Staff Sergeant," said Cooper. "If I raised the alarm, there'd be no light to see the threat. People would panic and start shooting blindly. I realized I had to accept the loss of my squad to save the camp, contain the infection, and eliminate the threat."

"So you fragged your own barracks," said Tate. "Then emptied an automatic weapon into it, just to be sure."

Cooper didn't flinch. He stood at attention, staring directly ahead. "Just to be sure, Staff Sergeant."

Tate looked long and hard at Cooper, who began feeling cracks in his stoic confidence.

Doubt swam through Cooper as images of long months in a brig flashed through his mind.

Then Tate relaxed his gaze. "Sergeant Wesson," he said. "Have these men fall out and clean themselves up, and have Private Cooper transfer his gear to his new barracks."

Cooper's shoulders sagged in relief, and found he could breathe again.

As Staff Sergeant Tate came over, Cooper noticed a corner of folded paper sticking out of his pocket, and quickly pushed it down, then came to attention as Tate looked him over with a nod.

"Welcome to your new unit."

Several soldiers sat behind the four rows of desks when Jack Tate walked into the briefing room, and all conversation abruptly stopped.

Tate's reputation around the base was that he was fair, tough, but a hard-liner. It was true that during his first year in the AVEF he expected his unit to know and adhere to military regulations, but few in the AVEF, including the Army at large, saw themselves as real military, and Tate's efforts were met with passive resistance.

His complaints to the CO died at his INBOX. Eventually, Tate gave up, but his reputation of being strictly 'by the book' endured.

Tate walked to the table at the front of the room, and leafed through a thick folder before beginning.

His jungle camos were weathered from hard use, but pressed and creased. His sleeves were uniformly rolled up to text-book standards, and the patch on the front of his ACUs had two extra rockers under the chevrons and a star in the center, signifying his recent promotion to sergeant major.

If anyone was surprised, they hid it behind expressions of stone.

The air conditioning hummed in the background, blunting most of the heat in the briefing room, but did little against the humidity.

In spite of the human touches, the room fell short in compensating for the style of bleak sterility common to the military, prisons and insane asylums.

Tate put down the folder, and spent a few seconds looking at each individual in the room.

"My name is Sergeant Major Jack Tate. I'm forming a new unit that will operate out of the Mortuary Affairs battalion, but will have very different duties. You've been selected for the opportunity to volunteer to be part of the unit."

Looking around the room, some of the faces were known to him, while others he was still trying to pin a name to. All eyes were on him, with a mixture of curiosity and respect of the rank.

"The information I will be speaking about is classified, which means you will not discuss what you hear with anyone. These missions are likely to be high risk. Your time outside the fence could last for days. If you're going to make it in this unit, you have to accept the demands expected of you. Consider things like calling in support a luxury. If things go wrong, or get rough, you are the only support you can count on. In short, I can promise you it will be dangerous."

Tate paused while scanning the room, looking at each face. He played a mental game, where he'd size up people and decide what they'd do. He thought of it as a game, but it was more of a skill, and had proved valuable in knowing who could be relied on and who was a weak link.

"Not everyone is cut out for this. There's no shame in accepting this about yourself. If you don't think this is for you, leave now."

After a moment, there was a squeak as a chair pushed away from a table, and a solider got up and left.

Tate smiled inwardly as he mentally put a check mark next to one of the soldiers he thought would leave.

"If you are still here because you're feeling curious, believe you're a badass, or are an adrenalin junky, I can guarantee before your first training is over, those feelings will be replaced by regret, exhaustion and pain. But it will be too late by then. Once you agree to be part of this unit, there is no getting out. There are no transfers, no loop holes, and if you're thinking you can go AWOL you will be the subject of a Casualty Notification to your next of kin, expressing your regrettable demise in the line of duty," said Tate, with a humorless smile. He wanted to drive home the seriousness of desertion, and by the expression around the room, he had succeeded.

Tate remained quiet, giving each soldier's mind plenty of room to run free. Silence was claustrophobic, spawning doubt and forcing it to feed on pride and ego.

After several minutes of quiet, another solider got up, and before they reached the door, four more got up and left.

After the door closed behind them, you could have heard a pin drop.

Tate was beginning to feel better about those still remaining. The ones he'd identified as not ready for the cut had gone, leaving him with a better sense of confidence in the remaining group.

Sergeant Wesson walked around the room, putting a form and pen in front of the remaining men and women.

"By signing this form," said Wesson, "you agree to the command structure, terms of classified information, risks and responsibilities of your duties and all terms stated. It is your responsibility to read and understand this document before signing."

"In short, your signature acknowledges that everything you do, see, and hear is classified. Understood?" asked Tate.

Everyone the room replied in one way or another.

Private Jared Cooper looked at the others around him as they busied themselves with filling out the forms. He didn't want to be there, but the decision was out of his hands.

Signing the form meant there was no turning back. If he was honest with himself, there was never a moment he could have turned back; from being tipped off to the simulated Vix attack on his barracks, following the instructions on how to beat it to getting Tate's attention.

Nearly from the moment he was assigned to the base, he had been someone's puppet, but the cost of cutting those strings would be devastating.

The process of weeding out people who weren't right for specialized missions was multi layered.

Tate had learned many of the 'tells', and seeing that Cooper was the one head not bent over his form was telling Tate that Cooper might not belong.

"What is it, Private Cooper?"

Cooper stiffened, not expecting to have been called out. He sat staring at Tate, caught in a conflict. If anyone knew why he was joining the unit, he could be court marshaled, or maybe shot. If he lost his nerve and walked out, the consequences would be a personal nightmare far worse than a firing squad.

"Private Cooper," said the sergeant major. "If you're looking for the door, it's located behind you. Otherwise, if you have a question, ask it."

Cooper nearly stuttered as his mind grasped for something to say. In the end, he only sat there, staring at Tate like a deer in headlights.

Tate was puzzled by Cooper's sudden appearance of doubt. He knew the private was green and needed training, but he was certain Cooper was a good fit for the unit; the private was struggling with something, and Jack was beginning to doubt his own judgment of Cooper.

Either way, this wasn't a therapy session. Either he was in, or out.

"Private Cooper, either you're trying to work up the courage to ask me out, or you believe I can read your mind. The answer to both is no."

Cooper grouped for an excuse, and threw out the first thing he could think of.

"Sorry, Sergeant Major. I'm not sure if my training is up to the types of missions I'm getting myself into," lied Cooper. He was scared; he knew what he was being forced into, but his self-doubt began to question if he could do it.

"No, Private. Before we go on our first mission, you're going to get additional training that's going to make boot camp look like nursery school."

Cooper mentally sighed with relief as another soldier raised his hand, shifting Tate's attention away from him.

Tate acknowledged the soldier, who stood. "Sergeant Major, if we're only fighting Victor Mikes, what's the big deal? We got all the training we need for a turkey shoot."

Tate walked to the front of the room and sat on the edge of his desk. "The training you got at boot was fine for doing janitor work, and that's what you've been doing, cleaning up the world's garbage. There's a back log of people waiting to sign up for that kind of duty, because they suck at life and think this is an easy way to make a buck using the system. They think all they have to do is slog through the jungle and shoot Vix. Three of four months later, half of those new grunts are dead from predators, snakes, poisonous spiders and frogs, infections, and disease. That uniform you're wearing makes you as much of a real soldier as a cape makes you Superman."

Jake Tate looked around the room with a mixture of melancholy and disappointment. His thoughts were never far from his fall of once being part of an elite combat unit to... this.

"You've never been in combat, or fought for your life. You have zero concept of how crippling stress under combat can be. Your training will prepare you to operate under the demanding conditions we can expect while in the field."

"Sergeant Major?" asked another private, visibly concerned. "Are we going to be in combat? Like, are we going to be shot at?"

Tate glanced at the name tape on the private's jacket.

"No, Private Fulton, but you will be trained to operate under stress. It's unpredictable out there. One minute, you're on a normal patrol, and the next minute, it's Oscar Sam Tango."

That got a chuckle from some of the seasoned grunts in the room, and helped break some of the tension.

"Oscar Sam Tango, Sergeant Major?" asked Fulton.

"It stands for 'Oh shit thirty', Private. It's a time you'll never see on a watch, but you'll know it the instant the second hand hits. Vix don't shoot back, but they're dangerous. You won't get combat training, but I'll give you training you can trust in."

Tate paused, giving everyone in the room time to ask other questions. "We start tomorrow at zero five hundred. You're dismissed."

Cooper stood to leave, and Tate walked over to him.

"Private Cooper, something is troubling you. If you're having self doubts, this is the time to leave them behind. If you can't, then this isn't the place for you."

Cooper instantly looked uncomfortable. "Yes, Sergeant Major," he said. "I, uh... Some of the guys in the room looked hard core. I'm just a rookie. I don't want to let them down."

"If you perform in the field like you did in that fake Vix attack, you'll fit in here," said Tate. "You can put on a uniform and sit behind a desk, but my guess is you wanted to be a soldier. A ship is safe in harbor, but that's not what ships are made for."

Cooper relaxed a bit, and smiled at the sergeant major. "Yeah, makes sense."

4

Cooper put on his cap and sunglasses as he stepped out of the briefing room, into the bright sunlight. The hot, moist air brought beads of sweat to his face almost instantly.

He started across the compound, scanning for any familiar face, pleased that only a few people were outside, and all of them strangers. Being out in the heat was something everyone tried to avoid when possible. Tarps and camo netting were hung up as cover, to shade the most often used pathways, and allowed Cooper to see who he may run into.

Glancing to see if he was noticed, he headed to a cluster of barracks a short distance away. Satisfied nobody was watching, he went inside the nearest barracks door, checking that it was empty.

Cooper took out his cell phone and dialed a number from memory. There was an audible click as the connection went through.

"Mr. Red, it's Jared Cooper. I'm in."

"I know who it is," said the person on the other end of the line. "Was there any trouble?"

"Trouble? No. Why do you think there was trouble?" Cooper tried to sound confident, but he was anything but.

The voice over the phone turned cold. "Don't lie to me! You want

49

me to special delivery another piece of your sister? What aren't you telling me?"

Coopers face lost all color as he flashed back to the day his family disappeared. He came home, finding only a note and a small white box on the table.

He would never be able to erase the image of the pale, bloody finger as it rolled in the box. The almost surrealistic candy-pink nail polish his little sister loved magnified the hideousness of the dark-red stub and white bone.

"No, don't do that." Cooper was overcome with guilt and despair. "I told you, it's fine. "I followed the instructions you gave me."

There was only silence on the other end of the line.

Cooper took a breath before going on. "It's fine," he said, sounding calmer. "I got into Sergeant Major Tate's squad."

"Good. His people aren't stupid. It's not likely they'll do anything when you're around until they get to trust you. Regardless. Give me daily reports on Tate, and any mention about your missions. You stick to the plan, and everything, and everyone, will be fine."

"I might not be..." A click told Cooper the other person had hung up.

He put his phone away, and looked around to reassure himself nobody had heard him.

The barracks was cooler inside, but Cooper was sweating more now than he'd been outside. He took a deep breath and wiped the tears from his eyes before stepping outside.

The next morning, Cooper arrived at the armory. As part of his assignment to his new unit, he needed a weapon.

He showed his requisition orders to the clerk. After checking the form against his list, the clerk unlocked the door and let him in.

"You're authorized for one rifle," said the guard, "from racks 'J' to 'L'. You can select a sidearm from rack 'O' and 'P'. Edged weapons are on rack 'W'. Got it?"

Cooper nodded to the guard and went inside. The darkness

blinked away as florescent lights flickered on, revealing row after row of weapons.

Cooper lingered, admiring some of the sleek, modern rifles with their laser sights, scopes and night vision optics, but his smile wilted when he reached the weapon rack marked 'J'.

Lined up in the rack were rifles that looked like something out of an old World War II movie; most had wooden stocks, that were scuffed and dinged from hard use. There were even bolt-action rifles, which Cooper had only seen in history books.

He picked up one of the rifles and blew on it, sending a fine cloud of dust curling into the air. He shook his head in disbelief that somewhere in the Army, an officer, who probably never even saw combat, would consider sending a soldier into harm's way with this museum relic.

"Finding your way around, Private?"

Cooper flinched, startled by the unexpected voice. He fumbled with the rifle, nearly dropping it; a cardinal sin in the army. Luckily he recovered it at the last moment.

He spun around to find Sergeant Major Tate behind him.

"Sergeant Major," said Cooper. "Good morning."

Tate him a good natured smile. "Good thinking getting here early, before the good ones are gone."

"Good ones, Sergeant Major?" said Cooper. "These weapons are junk. Why can't we get a newer weapon?"

"According to command, those are for real combat soldiers. Our role isn't deemed hazardous," said Tate sourly. "We sweep and clear an adversary that doesn't shoot back, so..."

Cooper looked at the rifle in his hands with doubt. "I've heard stories about guys getting ripped open because their rifle jammed and they got swarmed."

"Let me see that," said Tate, gesturing to Cooper's rifle.

Cooper handed it to Tate, who inspected it with crisp movements, like it was second nature.

"This is a Colt Bushmaster Gen-4. With this one, they finally worked out the touchy receiver. I don't think you'll have any trouble with jams. Whoever had it before you, took pretty good care of it. It's old, yeah, but it's light and easy to carry. It'll do the job."

Tate handed the rifle back to Cooper, who eyed it with new appreciation. "Thanks, Sergeant Major."

"Sure," said Tate. "See you at training."

Cooper took his rifle to the front desk, leaving Tate among the racks of near relics. He passed a few rows to the modern rifles, admiring the quality and design only a tested warrior could appreciate in a tool of combat.

He reached for one, but stopped himself, knowing it wasn't his to take.

"Not hazardous enough, they say. How would they know what hazardous is?"

The new unit was ending their second week of training, with Sergeant Wesson running them through their paces.

She didn't expect that she'd be running the training, but when Tate showed up two hours late on the first day, indifferent and with lukewarm energy, she realized that nothing was going to change.

She was confused and disappointed with Tate, because when he first approached her about joining the team he made it sound like a great opportunity to learn more skills, get away from the boredom of tedious patrols, and maybe springboard to another branch of the military; but two weeks later, and it was the same old Tate.

Wesson had more experience and field craft knowledge than the other team members, but not enough to fill an entire training course, and it was showing.

The training was becoming repetitive, and the unit was getting bored and losing focus. Wesson was spending half her time training, and the other half barking at someone for screwing around.

Tate wandered the training area with mild interest, giving someone a pointer or a bit of advice; he didn't see the harm in the team clowning around. They were just blowing off steam.

That night, Tate couldn't sleep. In the two years since his precious little girl was slaughtered, he had never told anyone about it until his encounter with Hewett at the Blue Orchid.

The memory of her innocent face hung like a loadstone around his neck; the weight of it had crushed his spirit. The irony of her death was sharp and achingly bitter. He'd devoted his life to protecting those he loved by defending his country, but when it mattered the most, he wasn't there for her. The knife bit even deeper, because he knew as he held his wife, racked with sorrow, he had nothing left to give, and he wasn't there for her, either.

He walked the darkened base until he finally felt his mind had quieted; maybe now, sleep would come.

Walking back to his quarters, he saw a light on at Wesson's apartment. Curious, Tate walked up to her door.

She'd thrown herself into training the new team, and it occurred to Tate he hadn't told her what a good job she was doing.

He thought he heard the television, and leaned his ear closer to the door. It wasn't the TV. She was crying. He knew what he was hearing, but he was so shocked it didn't seem real; he'd known Lori Wesson for the better part of a year, and he'd never seen her cry.

He stood there, lost in confusion, trying to figure out what was going on. Then, realization hit Tate with icy clarity.

It was him. He had neglected his responsibility of training the team, and let her carry the full weight on her shoulders until it had broken her to tears.

Once again, someone had relied on him, and he wasn't there for her. He stopped himself before his thoughts took him down that path for the millionth time.

He struggled for something to say, but no words came to his mind. After a moment, he turned away from the door and headed home, knowing he wouldn't find any sleep tonight.

Sergeant Wesson hoped the morning air would help clear her groggy head. Just to be sure, she'd swung by the base coffee shop.

The corporal on duty clearly appreciated the importance of coffee at four in the morning, and made it strong enough to beat-up a triple espresso and take its lunch money.

Wesson was sipping at her coffee when she arrived at the training area, and stopped in her tracks. Everywhere she looked, the team was hard at their exercises, with a seriousness she hadn't seen before. She did a double take, thinking she was in the wrong place.

"Good morning, Sergeant," said someone behind her.

Wesson turned, surprised to find Tate standing there. His PT uniform was already damp with sweat, and his face red from exertion.

"Did you have breakfast, yet?"

Wesson stammered as her answer and questions clashed over which would be spoken first. "No, Sergeant Major. What are you... I mean, why are...?"

"Get something to eat," said Tate, with a pensive smile. "You're going to need something besides that battery acid to get you through your training today."

Before she could reply, Tate walked into the training area, where a couple of team members were struggling to climb over an obstacle wall.

"Rosse, are you trying to climb my wall, or hump it?" yelled Tate.

"Climb it, top," puffed Rosse. "No way I work this hard to have sex with anything."

Wesson puzzled over Tate's change, but only briefly. Her own training soon occupied her full attention.

He wasn't perfect, at first. Tate hadn't undergone some amazing transformation, but little by little he worked himself into the role of Instructor, and in time their training improved.

Because they wouldn't be in combat, Tate's focus was on things like jungle field craft, squad communications, both verbal and in hand signals, and team building. Several of the members were from Tate's original squad and knew some of this, but all of them went through it so they could mentor the fresh recruits, adding a smack to the back of the head or a chewing out when needed.

Being rough on recruits was a tradition as old as time, and recruits, the smart ones, knew to accept it with a shut mouth.

Something that Cooper hadn't learned.

The team had been running a 'move and shoot' exercise for several hours. The exercise was set up to create a frantic and rapidly changing situation that required members to move together, while shooting pop up targets placed in every direction around them, and communicate and acknowledge each other's actions.

The exercise mirrored the stress and chaos that caused soldiers to become overwhelmed and get tunnel vision, or worse, mentally shut down.

The practice would start off fine, but as the intensity turned up, Cooper kept losing focus; making stupid mistakes. Each time they'd have to reset and start over.

It was their fifth time though it. The targets were springing up faster and closer to them as they tried to reach a safety zone.

One of the veterans, Specialist Brian Alkins, was on Cooper's right, calling out his right flank was blocked; they'd have to sweep left to avoid being cut off.

Cooper didn't respond, and stayed in his position. Frustrated with Cooper screwing up the exercise again, he shoved Cooper to clear his path.

Snapped out of his tunnel vision, Cooper flailed as he fell, catching Alkins by the belt.

Alkins tried to catch himself, but overbalanced and fell with Cooper into a tangled heap. Furious, he got up and yanked Cooper to his feet.

Cooper's bad performance in the exercises wasn't by accident. If he could get kicked off the team, he'd be useless to Mr. Red; there'd be no reason to hold Cooper's family. They'd be free, and he'd be free; as long as it didn't look like he quit, he'd be home free.

His thoughts were broken by Alkins yelling in his face.

"Open your damn ears when I'm talking to you," shouted Alkins, and slapped Cooper upside his head.

It wasn't a hard hit, but for Cooper it amounted to the final straw. Months of living in fear for his family, guilt and frustration boiled over, and Cooper saw red.

He drove at Alkins with everything he had, who deftly turned away his attack.

"You want to think twice about doing that again, buddy." Alkins was thoroughly capable of beating Cooper to a pulp, but Cooper didn't care; he was desperate to stop feeling like a victim.

He launched himself at Alkins, when someone grabbed his shirt from behind and wrenched him off his feet.

Cooper landed on his back with a grunt, having the wind knocked out of him.

Tate stood over him, leveling a hard look at Alkins. "I think we're done here, Specialist, don't you?"

Alkins shifted his glare from Cooper to Tate, then let his hand relax from the white-knuckled fist he was about to use on Cooper, and dusted himself off.

"Kick him, Top. He's gonna get someone killed... if he don't die first." Alkins left, and the rest of the squad went back to training, leaving a lot of space between them and Tate.

Cooper got up slow, feeling the ache of a hard landing.

"I'm sorry, Sergeant Major. I screwed up. Maybe Alkins is right."

If Tate didn't know better, he thought Cooper sounded relieved. There was something going on deep below the surface with this private.

Tate knew Cooper had potential, and didn't want to give up on him just yet.

"What's going on with you?"

The question surprised Cooper, catching him completely off guard. He was expecting to get chewed out then, he hoped, marched off the team.

"You handled that surprise drill in the barracks like you were made for this team. Ever since then you look like you're half-assing every training exercise."

"I don't know," said Cooper. "I got scared back in the barracks. It was just reaction and I got lucky. I thought I could bluff my way through training, get a quick promotion to a desk assignment." He shrugged his shoulders in a feeble gesture of apology.

Tate didn't believe a word out of Coopers mouth, but he didn't have time for games. "If you want out, then you're out."

Those words were sweet relief to Cooper, and he began to feel salvation spreading though him; his family would be free soon.

"For security reasons, you'll be reassigned out of the country," said Tate.

"I understand," said Cooper, faking disappointment.

If Cooper wanted out, Tate would grant him his wish, but he resented being jerked around by this private, and didn't have any qualms returning the favor.

"I don't think you do. As the NCO, it's my opinion you purposely sabotaged your training with the desired result of being expelled from the team, and your record will reflect that."

The color drained from Cooper's face. Mr. Red had demonstrated he knew things that happened on the base; Cooper imagined Red might have spies there. The slightest twinge on Mr. Red's spider web, and he'd know about it before the sun had gone down.

If the Sergeant Major wrote on Cooper's record that he was deliberately getting himself kicked out, it was guaranteed Mr. Red would learn about it.

Mr. Red was only a voice to him, but it was a smothering, claustrophobic voice he couldn't escape. They'd never met, but Mr. Red knew all about Cooper. Even more frightening was how he knew what Cooper was doing all the time.

Verging on panic, it took all of Cooper's self-control not to grab Tate.

"No," he pleaded. "I mean, I wouldn't do that. I mean, I'm not trying to get kicked out." His plan was careening out of control, and on the brink of getting himself and his family killed. His mind scrambled for something to say that could veer him away from the cliff he was heading towards.

"Private Cooper, are you jerking me around?" asked Tate, completely confused. "Are you telling me I didn't hear you just say you were bluffing your way through training, or was that my imagination? Are you telling me I'm losing my mind, Private? Is that what you're saying?"

"No, Sergeant Major, that's not what I'm saying."

"What's that, Private? I can't hear you over the sound of your own bullshit."

"No, Sergeant Major," shouted Cooper, snapping to attention. "It wasn't bullshit. I was mad about Alkins, and feeling like everyone's pushing me around. Nobody wants me on the team, and I said what I thought they wanted me to say... to get rid of me, Sergeant Major."

Tate leaned in, locking eyes with Cooper. "Private, I decide who stays and who goes. That's my job, not yours. Your job, everyone's job here, is to drop their bullshit and operate as a team. This training and everyone in it is supposed to be hard on you. It grinds away the lies and bullshit everyone pretends to be, until all that's left is the bone. When that's all that's left, *then* everything else falls into place. The skill, the knowledge, the teamwork. Then it happens. That process can't happen because you're fighting it."

Tate stood back and folded his arms across his chest. "So, what's it going to be, Private?"

"I understand, Sergeant Major," Cooper blurted. "I'll stay if you let me. Just give me to the end of the week to prove I'm committed. I will be as good any one here."

Tate crunched his thoughts about what to do with Cooper. There were a lot of conflicts within him, and that gave him some serious doubt, but it also presented a challenge; something Tate hadn't had in a long time.

He could cut the private loose, but that felt like the easy way out. He pushed his finger into Cooper's chest.

"You've got your head so far up your own ass you don't know the meaning of good. When I was a fresh recruit, I thought I was good. I had the speed, reflexes, and all the answers. I didn't have to try, so I didn't take training seriously. I wanted to kick in heads and be a badass. The rest of my squad thought I was a class A prick. One day, we're going through hand-to-hand combat, and my squad decided this was their chance to bust me up, and they didn't hold anything back. I admit I <u>was</u> a class A prick, and had it coming. I should have lost, but I young, tough and stubborn. I beat every one of them. It wasn't that I was a better fighter. It was just that I could suck up more pain than they could. My Drill Instructor didn't care I was thrashing these guys, but he sure as hell cared that I was half-assing my way through his course."

Tate paused, smiling as the memory played out in his mind. "Suddenly, the DI was nose to nose with me and I'm thinking I'm in for a first rate chewing. Instead, he says, 'Private Tate, I've seen guys like you, before. They're good. Really good. I'm gonna reassign you to their detail. Keeping you with your squad is a waste of your talents. I'm picking you up oh five hundred tomorrow.', and without another word he walks off."

Cooper was looking at Tate like he was Superman. "Oh man," he said. "You were getting into the elite, right?"

"Something like that," said Tate. "The next morning, oh five hundred sharp, the DI drives up. We're driving for about 30 minutes and the whole time the DI is telling me how he told them all about me last night, and how I'm going to fit right in with these guys. The sun's started to throw some light over the horizon when we crested a hill, and he stopped and got out. I followed him, looking around. 'There they are.' I look where he pointed and saw it is a grave yard. I stood there trying to make sense of what was going on.

"He took me down into that graveyard and walked me passed one headstone after another. 'Private Ryan Beal. Private Scott Everett. Private Napier, Hedley, McAvoy, Cole, Henries, Janes...' He'd written the same thing on the side of each headstone.

"'All of these guys thought they were good, just like you. I stood by every one of their caskets as they got lowered into the ground, just like I'm gonna stand next to yours. I wrote on their headstones, just like I'm gonna write on yours, because being good got them killed, just like it's gonna kill you.'

"The thought of seeing my headstone lying in a neat row with all those others brought home the reality of my mortality. I left all my bullshit behind in that grave yard. Nobody was ever going to write on my headstone."

"What was it?" Cooper asked. "What did he write?"

Tate looked at Cooper, searching for sincerity, hoping this wasn't wasted on the kid. "Good is the enemy of great."

Cooper didn't say anything, but his expression told Tate the private understood exactly what he meant. Cooper could stay in the unit, and Tate knew he'd be all right.

5

BRIEFING

I t had been three weeks since training had finished, and Tate was getting impatient. He knew their first mission was coming, but he didn't expect it to take this long. He wasn't a stranger to how slow the military moved, but the colonel made it sound like his group of suits were chaffing at the bit for Tate's team to become operational. It had been a long time since the colonel had been on the base, and Tate was beginning to wonder if something had changed. He'd have to wait until they needed him, but he hoped it was soon, before they started losing their edge; it had been a while for him, too, and he was feeling a restless energy building up inside him.

Twelve days before, Colonel Hewett had walked into Tate's office and placed a briefcase on his desk.

All his time in Spec Ops, Tate's operation briefings had been handled by his commanding officer; usually a lieutenant. Tate guessed that cutting out that many levels of the command chain meant this was classified on a level a lot higher than he first thought. Tate came to attention and saluted.

"At ease, Sergeant Major." Hewett cocked his head slightly, looking at Tate. "Have you lost weight?"

"A little, sir," said Tate.

"Training will do that to you," said the colonel, as he took a chair.

He opened the briefcase taking out a mission packet, and put it in front of Tate.

Tate opened it, and briefly scanned through the contents. Inside were maps, sat pictures, and a thick file on someone named Ben Fin. He sounded familiar, but Tate couldn't put his finger on why.

Going through the packet, he discovered multiple folders of information. "It'll take me a while to get through all of this, sir."

The colonel reached into his briefcase and took out a newspaper. "I got time."

He opened the paper and leaned back as if Tate wasn't there.

A red flag went up in Tate's head; full bird colonels didn't cool their heels waiting on Sergeant Majors. When the military found a process that worked, it became a standard operating procedure. The rest of the world would call it a ritual, and the Army loved its rituals. Departing from the SOP was seriously frowned upon; the Army had a process for running classified operations, and this wasn't it. This had the feel of somebody outside the Army making the rules, and whoever they were had enough clout to make a colonel sit in a Sergeant Major's office, playing babysitter.

If the colonel was going to give him the time to read through all the intel, he wouldn't complain. Experience had made Tate a convert to the edict 'the devil's in the details'; those seemingly unimportant things had a nasty way of coming back on you at the worst time. It had been a long time since he'd read a mission packet, and he was out of practice, so Tate took his time.

It was about two hours later when Tate closed the last folder, and neatly stacked it on the others.

"You can keep all the intel, except the folder on Fin," said the colonel from the other side of the newspaper. "Ask your questions."

Tate slid the folders back in the envelope and tamped it on his desk, before tying the packet closed.

"Sir, this says we're collecting intel from an American ambassador's vacation house. I thought we were going to be doing recons, search and clear. Ops like that."

The colonel folded the paper, stretching as he sat up with a grunt. "This is the mission

future missions hinge on. What you're retrieving contains critical locations, key codes, and other vital information. So, you understand the importance of making this a successful op?"

Tate asked for details the mission packet didn't answer. Abort procedures, possible difficult terrain, etc., and took notes, with the colonel's permission, but there was an unmistakable feeling that the colonel knew more than he was saying; this wasn't new to Tate, and he told himself to ignore it.

The 'higher ups' typically compartmentalized information.

An hour later, they finished up. The colonel stood and Tate followed suit.

Hewett picked up the folder on Ben Fin. "Whatever you find is 'eyes only'. You and your team aren't cleared. Everything goes from his safe into the grab-bag without anyone reading it."

"Understood, Colonel. Is there anything else?"

Hewett took out a cell phone from his pocket and put it on Tate's desk. "This is a secure phone. Anytime we need to talk privately, use this. If nothing else comes up, we'll talk again after the mission."

"Sounds good, sir," said Tate, saluting.

The colonel returned his salute, then walked out.

There was a nagging feeling in the back of Tate's mind that this *was* like other ops he'd run; the kind where he was only getting half the story, and the other half was where the real danger waited.

He shook off the thought and dialed his phone.

"Sergeant Wesson, assemble the team for a mission briefing at ten hundred hours tomorrow morning. Thanks."

That morning, the squads gathered for their first official mission briefing. The room was filled with an unspoken excitement.

Everyone had a folder with 'Classified' stamped on the outside in large, bold letters.

Private Cooper was just opening his folder when he realized none of the veterans had touched theirs. Instead, their attention was on Sergeant Major Tate.

Cooper hurriedly closed his folder and nudged it away.

Tate walked up to a white screen and put a thick folder down on the table next to him.

"Good morning. I'm going to cover the high points of this mission, and I'd like you to hold your questions until I'm finished. Each of you has a folder with mission details, your unit assignments, radio frequencies, call signs and timetables. You will study and memorize the mission intel forwards and back, before you put a boot on the helicopter skids come deployment day. As you saw by the big, red letters on your folders, this mission is classified. You do not discuss anything related to this mission with anyone outside this room."

He paused to look around the room, making sure he had everyone's attention, and picked up a pointer-stick.

"Sergeant Wesson, let's get this show started."

A moment later, Wesson turned on a digital projector from the back of the room. On the screen appeared a photo of a heavy, balding man in a suit, sitting at a desk with the American flag staged behind him. It was a typical publicity photograph, where everyone had perfect teeth and completion.

"This is, or was, Ben Fin. Before he went missing, at the time of the outbreak, he was the American Ambassador to Colombia. Just prior to the country's collapse, Ambassador Fin was in possession of valuable intel."

The image on the screen changed to an aerial view of a city. The image zoomed in to a devastated area of destroyed buildings.

"Sat recon of the American embassy in Bogota shows a pile of smoking rubble, and it's believed anything of value was destroyed along with the building. Any hope of salvaging that intel was written off. Until..."

Appearing on the screen next to Tate was a satellite image of the west coast of Columbia.

Tate zoomed in to a twenty-mile area of fractured coast, speckled with small atolls and river inlets. The dense blanket of trees crowded up to the blue waters edge.

Tate zoomed the image, revealing a patch of gleaming white beach with a single dock perched over the water. At the other edge of the beach was a large house with a swimming pool and tennis court. A wall, or fence, bordered the entire area, extending a short ways into the water.

Tate tapped the image with his stick. "Before the reanimated shit hit the fan, this was the vacation villa of Mr. Fin. It's located about twenty-seven clicks from the city Buenaventura. There's strong evidence that Fin kept copies of files in a personal safe, and yes, that's where we're going. Questions?"

Tate pointed to one of the hands that went up around the room. "Rosse."

Before the prisons had been emptied to refill the rapidly depleted ranks of the military, Tyler Rosse had been a career prison guard. He didn't have a problem with rules as long as he was enforcing them. He did have a problem with authority, and little respect for some "pussy" giving him orders. The other NCOs were either fed up or frightened of him, and eagerly recommended Tate take him.

Tate had watched Rosse before approaching him for the team. Rosse wasn't stupid, and his barrel chest wasn't just for show. He displayed the physical and mental skills for the missions Tate's team would be pulling. His obstinate attitude toward authority didn't phase Tate.

In Rosse's case, he resented anyone in authority who hadn't earned their position. It was an attitude Tate could appreciate from both sides of the fence, and was quick to cement in Rosse's mind that his new NCO was firmly at the top of the food chain.

"All of our forward bases are north and east of Colombia," said Rosse. "That looks about three hundred mikes south of any reconed territory. If the brass wanted to get rid of us, they could just discharge us."

Tate smiled at the easy laughter in the room. In spite of the excitement, the team was becoming comfortable enough to joke with him.

"You don't get out of the Army that easy. Here's where it gets fun."

The satellite image pulled back and shifted down the coast to a wide inlet. Where the inlet broke up into several rivers was an island city.

"This is the city of Buenaventura, and most of the territory surrounding it was prime real-estate for the drug cartel. Back when there was a cartel, the U.S. government tasked The Drug Enforcement Agency, which has gone the way of the Dodo bird, with stopping drug smuggling into the U.S. As part of that operation, the DEA established several paramilitary fire support bases throughout South America, which they would execute raids from. We're going to be airlifted to this river about four and a half mikes west of Buenaventura, then travel two miles on foot to an abandoned DEA base, designated check point Phoenix, which has two fast boats. From there, we're going to take a fast boat along the coast to our objective. There we'll search the location for our intel, and return along the same route we used, where we will extract via helo."

The projector turned off, and Tate leaned against the table behind him. "Questions?"

The first hand up was Sergeant Monkhouse. He was the team's engineer. What he lacked in conventional training he made up for with the ability of improvising solutions from nearly anything at hand. "You said that base had boats?" said Monkhouse. "Are they working?"

"I doubt it, but that's why I picked you as our engineer, Sergeant Monkhouse," said Tate.

"Hey, Top," said Monkhouse, leaning back in his chair. "I'm good. Okay, better than most, but even I wouldn't bet all my chips I can fix them. We don't know their condition *and* we don't even know if that camp has been looted. Without replacement parts, those boats and us aren't going anywhere."

"Sergeant Monkhouse," said Tate, "do I detect a note of skepticism regarding the reliability of the intel we've been given?" Quiet laughter rolled around the room.

"He's right," said Tate. "No matter how solid intel looks, you should never rely on it until your boots are on the ground and you see for yourself. If you go into a situation feeling safe and secure because intel says so, you're going to drop your guard and get careless. At best, intel is an advisement. We roll the dice. If the boats don't work, we try something else. This team isn't about aborting the moment something goes wrong. We get the mission done."

"Why don't they drop us on the guy's front lawn?" asked Rosse. "Seems like a lot of extra work on our part."

"A couple of reasons," replied Tate. "The helo crew isn't cleared to know our mission, or our final destination. They don't even know about the DEA base. Another is, like you pointed out, this area is completely unexplored. We could get dropped into a heard of Vix and not even know it until half your arm is eaten off. On the bright side, here's your chance to get out on the water and out of the jungle."

"I don't know how to swim," groused Rosse. "And I ain't wearing one of them stupid looking life preserver things."

Tate let out a small sigh. "Then I suggest that everybody here that Rosse owes money to, collect it before the mission, or you might not ever get it back." Good-natured laughter rolled around the room as another hand went up.

"Suller," said Tate, pointing to one of the raised hands.

"What's our unit name?" asked Suller.

"Until we get our official designation it'll be Rover," said Tate. That brought a groan from the room. "Yeah, I know. But we won't have to live with the dog jokes for long. I promise, I'll get us a better name."

Tate decided to wrap it up and let them get on with their mission prep. "Remember, this is classified. We lift off tomorrow at oh six hundred."

6

CHECK POINT PHOENIX

The sun was breaking over the treetops as Private Cooper jogged into the mission assembly area. The rest of the squad was there. The guys who were in Tate's earlier unit were talking in their own group. Most of the newbies to the unit were talking in groups, trying to look bored, but their quick glances for any signs of change in the veteran's actions betrayed their nerves.

Cooper dumped his combat pack next to the others, lined up in a neat row, then looked around, unsure what to do with himself.

He played over the anxiety of last night's events. He had covertly scanned the mission documents and transmitted them to Mr. Red, using a secret cell phone. That was nerve racking enough, but then he received a demand to call Mr. Red immediately.

"Your mission's in the morning, and I'm just getting this now?" snapped Mr. Red.

Cooper was scared that Mr. Red would take out his fury on his family, and hastily explained they'd only just been given the mission briefing.

"They like to keep things close to the vest," said Mr. Red. "This'll take some fast planning."

"Planning?" Cooper said, confused. "We're lifting off in a few hours. There's nothing I can do."

"Huh? Ignore that. I was thinking out loud," said Red. There was an uncharacteristic pause as Cooper heard the sound of papers rustling over the phone.

"Uh, look, I want you to get me copies of those documents you're going after."

Tension tightened around Cooper's chest, and he gripped the phone as his mind raced through the ramifications of Red's demand.

"Do you even know what you're asking me to do? Why are you doing this to me? I'm nobody."

"Exactly," said Mr. Red. "That's why we picked you. To everyone else you're just another face in the crowd. There's nothing special about you, and you're new. People are more likely to give you the benefit of the doubt for making mistakes."

"It'll never work. Don't you understand? There's no way they're going to leave me alone with whatever we find. I'm not even supposed to see them. They're going to catch me, maybe shoot me on the spot."

Cooper was quickly working himself into a panic, but Mr. Red only heard excuses.

"Do you know how embarrassed I get every time I have to explain to my superiors why you keep screwing with us?" said Red. "It hardly leaves anytime to look after your family. Come to think of it, I can't remember. Did I feed them yesterday, or was it the day before? Your sister, what is she, five? They're always so hungry at that age, but those are the formative years."

Cooper couldn't see a way out. His surrender to Mr. Red's demands where his family's life line, but no matter how hard he tried, risk and disaster loomed over him; he was a living lie to everyone but the man that held his family hostage, and even he didn't care if Cooper lived or died.

So, Mr. Red would send him on a suicide mission. He'd be caught by Tate and shot on the spot. He would die, then so would his family.

That's it. I die no matter what happens. If I'm gonna die, why drag it out? Let's get it over with.

Feeling like there was nothing to lose Cooper embraced his reckless anger and for the first time in a long time, felt like a free man.

"What kind of sick bastard tortures a kid? First you cut up my sister, then you starve her? And for what? Some documents? How about I just ask Tate if I can borrow them to give to the guy that's blackmailing me? Huh? No, I got it. I'll just kill my whole squad. Sounds like something you'd like, right? And then I'll drive right up to your front door and put the papers in your hands. But you know that won't happen, because as soon as I try to steal those papers someone'll put a bullet in my head, so why wait? I'll shoot myself right now. Either way, I'm going to die, and then you'll kill my family."

Alarms were beginning to go off in Mr. Red's mind. His ambition to get those documents had made him push Cooper too far. He'd lose his only asset in Tate's unit, his chance at the papers; not to mention the questions Cooper's suicide would cause. Anyone looking into it would find the encrypted cell phone, and *did Cooper keep a journal, or write notes about any of this?*

Alarm bells went off in Mr. Red's head. He had underestimated how unstable Cooper was, and had to work fast to bring him back from the edge.

Mr. Red decided Cooper was too much of a risk, and after he delivered those papers he'd have Cooper killed. He had another asset within that military base. One he could rely on to sanitize Cooper's belongings, so there'd be nothing to tie him to Mr. Red.

But first things first.

Mr. Red took a deep breath, thinking quickly how to defuse Cooper.

"You're right. This whole situation is terrible. I'm going to tell you something, but it's just between you and me, you understand? If anyone knew, we'd all be dead. You, me, your family..." Mr. Red paused before going on. "Your family's, fine, okay? They're fine. Nobody cut up your sister. We got the finger from a morgue. The people I work for aren't sadistic, they don't believe in torture. But, Cooper, they do believe in killing, *if* they're forced to. That's why we need to work together. As long as I can tell my boss everything's going according to plan, your family stays secure, watching TV, eating pizza. But you have to help me help them. I know what I'm asking you to do is dangerous, but it's for the right reasons. Believe me when

I tell you, we're on the same side. You're serving this country and so am I."

Mr. Red waited a moment to let his words take root. "So, can I count on you, Jared?"

Cooper had calmed down, let himself listen to Mr. Red. He wanted to believe Mr. Red was telling the truth, even though his suspicion told him they were all lies; but he saw a chance and he took it.

"Yes, I'll try."

"Come on," said Mr. Red. "Try? After all this special training you got, I know you'll be good at this."

"Good is the enemy of great," said Cooper.

"Yeah," said Mr. Red, sounding encouraged. "Yeah, that's the spirit. I'm glad to see you're on board with this. Good is the enemy of great. I'm going to remember that one."

It was the first time Cooper felt like he was talking to a person and not a monster threatening death over his family. He didn't know how long it would last, but he saw an opportunity to find out more about Red and went for it.

"Why didn't you just ask?" he said. "You could've told me you're trying to do something good, but dangerous, and asked me to help."

"It's not that simple," said Mr. Red. "A long time ago people thought surgery was evil, or witchcraft. People couldn't see beyond the blood being spilt. It's the same now, but on a global scale. To save lives, blood has to be spilled and most can't see beyond the blood. I can. I accept the spilling of blood because I know it'll lead to a better world. A new world."

Mr. Red was confident the blending of lies and truth had maneuvered Cooper back into his pocket. He was being honest when he said his bosses didn't believe in torture, but Mr. Red did. It was a hugely effective tool, but one that he'd have to hold in reserve now that Cooper was so fragile.

The line went dead, and Cooper felt a wash of relief and doubt flow through him. Had he gone too far? Did his outburst just make him disposable?

He deliberated if he should call back, but decided he might just make things worse. His thoughts were broken as someone tugged on his sleeve.

"Private Cooper, I'm talking to you." Sergeant Wesson gave him an annoyed look. "Have you double checked your combat pack according to the mission load out?"

"Yes, Sergeant," blurted Cooper, a little too loudly. "two hundred rounds of ammo. Two canteens of water. Four pairs of socks..."

"I don't need to hear the whole list," said Wesson. Her expression softened slightly, and she gave Cooper a once over.

"Don't go into this mission nervous. You won't do anyone any good that way. If you have a question, or aren't sure what to do, let me know. We do our mission and we come home, simple as that."

Cooper only nodded. He wasn't thinking about the mission at the moment. He was thinking how pretty Lori Wesson was when she wasn't yelling at him.

He was terrified that the way he looked at her would give him away, because she would kill him on the spot. So he did his best to hide it behind his poker face; it must have worked, because she nodded with approval and walked off.

The mood of the assembly area shifted from casual boredom to excitement as the pilots kicked on the Black Hawk engines. The hum of the turbines climbed to a steady whine. Soon it was joined by a deeper hum, as the rotor blades slowly started to rotate.

The crew chief stood outside near the nose of the helicopter, visually monitoring the startup. The rotating blades quickly gained speed until they were a blur. The rotor wash buffeted the soldiers and blew unattended gear off the assembly platform.

Satisfied with his visual inspection, the crew chief slid open the rearward cargo door and gave a thumbs-up to Sergeant Major Tate.

Tate returned the gesture, then waved the squad forward and pointed to the open cargo door.

The squad lined up with their combat packs slung over their shoulders, as the crew chief directed each squad member to a jump seat, instructing them what to do with their combat pack and weapon.

With everyone on, Tate grabbed the metal frame of the bench seat and pulled himself inside. He put on the headset, and the engine noise was instantly brought down to a manageable level.

Across from him, the crew chief did a final inspection of the squad and gear. He switched the channel on his flight helmet, and his voice crackled through Tate's earphones.

"Good morning, Sergeant Major," said the crew chief. "I'm Sergeant Gibbs. I'll be your crew chief for this ride. Our target landing zone is two hundred and eighty eight miles, give or take, and our travel time will be about an hour and fifteen minutes."

"Thank you, Sergeant," said Tate. He had familiarized himself with the flight details the night before, but appreciated having a crew chief who didn't treat everyone like cargo.

Tate had studied weather, times, distance, and a long list of other mission details until he knew them by heart. His years as top tier operator had taught him the power of knowing every detail about a mission.

Tate pushed the headset off one ear and yelled over the noise to his squad. "Ready?"

Everyone answered with a thumbs-up.

After a short glance, the crew chief nodded.

Reseating the headset, Tate heard him talking to the pilots.

"We're secure and you are clear to go," said Gibbs.

The whine of the turbines climbed to a roar, and the Black Hawk lifted off. Soon they were hovering above the camp. The nose of the helicopter tipped forward, and the ground below slipped by with nearly no sensation of movement.

The squad craned their necks to take in the view. Below them rolled an unbroken canopy of lush green that stretched away into the misty horizon.

The stillness of the landscape gave a sense of tranquility, but Tate wasn't deceived by the facade. Beneath the blanket of green, life ranged from miserable to lethal.

He smiled to himself, amused by his own cynicism. *You can't even let yourself appreciate a good view, can you?* he thought to himself.

Eventually, the green terrain changed to a deep blue, as they broke over the ocean. With it brought a cool breeze, giving relief to the soldiers sweating under their full combat load.

Tate stared off into the misty horizon, as memories drifted through his mind of his life before everything changed. He thought of the men he called 'brother', and the missions that bonded them together; a bond Tate thought could only be broken by death.

It had been two years since he had closed the door on that life, but he still thought of his brothers with a mixture of regret and guilt; they'd been a part of his life nearly from the time he'd joined the military. They had been there on his wedding day, the birth of his daughter, Jesse, and the day he got word she'd been killed.

Even if he'd wanted, he couldn't hide the devastation that sunk its claws into his spirit and ripped it from his chest. All meaning had been shredded from his life, leaving it a colorless wasteland.

For a year he'd poured into keeping himself busy, thinking that one day he'd wake up and begin to feel normal again, but that feeling never came. His wife had struggled, too, but was incredibly strong; she could see the devastation and guilt crushing down on Tate. The more she loved him, the less worthy he felt of her. He was lost, without any thought what to do.

The answer had come to him one night while staring at the ceiling in the shroud of darkness; a voice of clarity that told him he had to leave. Right then and there.

The groaning weight he had felt relentlessly crushing him since his precious girl had been ripped from him seemed to crumble away.

Ten minutes later, he was driving through the night. The direction didn't matter, only distance. With every mile, he felt the tendrils of despair loosening their hold on him.

The next few months were like air to a drowning man. He was a blank slate. Settling down in Texas, nobody knew him and nobody cared. He constructed a new past, and with it Tate was created.

He was surprised at how easy it was, stepping into a new life, trailing none of the ghosts of his past; but that had all been a lie. His past was with him, patiently searching for the chink in his fantasy, and one night, it found it.

With a hunger, his past chewed through his delusions of a new start. He dreamt of his wife, anguishing alone, deserted by the man who had made vows as he slipped on her wedding ring. He saw his friends fighting for their lives, undefended by the man who had taken oaths to protect them with his life.

Reality had crashed down on him like a massive granite wall, and he awoke, gasping, as regret and shame stared him in the face, denying him from looking away from the truth that he had deserted his friends and wife.

A burst of static scattered this thoughts. "Hey, Top," said Sergeant Monkhouse. "That jungle looks like something from one of those dinosaur movies. What would you do if you ran into a T-Rex?"

Bret Monkhouse was one of the original members of Tate's squad when he first started in Mortuary Affairs, and he was glad to have him. His specialty was as the engineer of the squad; whether it was a makeshift bridge, demolitions, or booby traps, Monkhouse could do it.

No matter how bad something went, he'd always have a smile. Tate decided long ago it was because Monkhouse knew that sooner or later, he'd get to blow something up, and that cheered him up all day long.

Tate pushed back the shrouds of emotions, and brought himself back into the present moment.

"Monkhouse, where do you come up with this stuff?"

"I'm a renaissance man, Top. I think about all kinds of things. So, what would you do?"

"I'd run like a bat out of Hell."

Monkhouse laughed. "Get real, Sergeant Major. You're not exactly in the kind of shape to outrun a T-Rex."

"I'm not in any shape to outrun a T-Rex, but I'll bet good money I can outrun a mouthy sergeant," chuckled Tate.

The rest of the team laughed.

"Heads up, Sergeant Major," said the crew chief. "We're twenty minutes out."

"Thanks," said Tate. "All right, squad, you heard it. Last check before we're feet on the ground."

Everyone went through their individual examination of their gear, until the last of them signaled in with a 'good to go' thumbs up.

The air became moist and hot as the Black Hawk banked to the left, leaving the blue ocean behind and cutting inland. The pilot began following a meandering river, which Tate remembered from his map was near their insertion point.

As if reading his thoughts, the Black Hawk gently flared, then came to a hover over a break in the jungle near the bank of the river.

The crew chief reached out and grabbed the fast-rope, just below where it was anchored to a metal brace on the outside of the helicopter. He checked that the coil of rope wasn't tangled with anything and kicked it out the door, watching it unwind as it fell to the ground.

The crew chief flipped up a plastic cover on the bulkhead near his seat that protected the quick-release button for the fast rope. This had become a necessary precaution after a helicopter and everyone on it was lost when a soldier was repelling down the rope, and a couple of Vix had appeared.

The soldier had stopped halfway down the rope while his squad shot at the Vix from the helo. The sounds of gunfire attracted a hoard of Vix from everywhere. The soldier had dangled on the rope like bait above a swarming meat grinder. He was screaming for help, his hands shaking were shaking with fatigue, as his friends tried to pull him up. It was a tug of war they couldn't win. The Vix swarmed the rope. Their sudden weight began pulling the helo. The pilot panicked, over corrected, and swung into the trees. The rotor shattered spraying fragments like bomb shrapnel. The ones who died in the crash were lucky.

After that, helicopter crews didn't wait for a response to retro-fit a quick-release switch. They did it themselves, giving new life to the adage 'Every solution breeds new problems'.

The problem here was that not everyone was a mechanical engineer. Some of the jury-rigged rope couplings broke under the weight and stress of a fully loaded combat soldier resulting in people falling to their deaths.

Helicopter crews were some of the tightest knit families in the military, and while they honestly felt bad for the lost soldiers, their attitude was 'better them than us'.

Fortunately, the Army approved the idea, issued a reliable quick-release system, and prevented further injuries.

With a thumbs-up signal, Lori Wesson moved to the door and sat down with her feet over the edge.

As the Unit Automatic Rifleman, she was the first on the ground. With her LM-948, she could chew up a mob of Vix without breaking a sweat.

Built off a polymer/teflon frame, the .338 caliber light machine gun dissipated heat, making it possible to fire magazine after magazine without the risk of deforming the barrel. The high-energy rounds chemically reacted on impact. Hitting an object, the slug deformed into a metal wad and instantly hardened in that shape. The slug's combination of shape and velocity created an annihilating impact that would penetrate through multiple soft targets.

It was jaw dropping to see in action.

The crew chief reached out and pulled the rope to her, then put his hand on her shoulder while she got her grip.

She nodded she was ready and he patted her shoulder, signaling she could go. She swung out and instantly started her slide down, while the next soldier got in position.

Soon it was Tate's turn and he wasted no time in getting to the rope. The sound of the helicopter was thumping in his ears, but his time in Special Forces had taught him how to push the distraction out of the way.

He scanned the area from above for the last time, as he felt the crew chief's hand pat his shoulder twice.

Tate leaned out and was free of the helicopter. The rotor wash beat down on him as he slid down the rope.

He felt like the jungle was reaching up for him, and as he passed the bright-green canopy, he was being swallowed into its dark, fetid belly.

His boots hit soil and the illusion passed. The others had already set up a defensive perimeter, while the last of the unit left the safety of the Black Hawk.

After a final headcount, Tate waved off the helicopter, which banked away; its thumping fading into the distance.

Everyone stayed in position and listened for any tell tale clue that the sound of the helicopter had attracted any Vix.

Slowly, the sounds of the jungle returned, and nothing more. Soon the air was alive with the noise of insects and animals.

Satisfied they hadn't attracted any Vix, Tate keyed up his mic. "Let's head out. Wesson is on point. Single file."

They'd hardly touched down, and Tate's camo uniform was already damp with sweat.

They moved into the jungle, and were soon swallowed by the vegetation.

While several of the squad members had been in Tate's last platoon, three soldiers were new to him, including Private Cooper.

Tate had spread out the greener soldiers among the more seasoned members to keep an eye on them, and catch any mistakes before they happened.

Cooper had trained for this, but this was too real. The reality that he was on a real mission with no 'do overs' began to overwhelm him.

He'd been out in the jungle before, but everyone knew the area was secure; the worst that could happen was getting chewed out for doing something stupid. But here, now, he felt he was walking a razors edge, and was a hairs breath away from dying, or getting someone else killed. There wasn't a safety net out here.

The jungle crowded in on the team, making it impossible to see anything lurking just an arm reach away. The closeness made the air stale, heavy and thick.

The jungle growth they couldn't push through had to be hacked, and the sound of the chopping echoed like a signal announcing their presence.

A screech tore over their heads, and the team instantly stopped and crouched, except for Cooper, who froze.

His eyes were wide with fear, and his gaze darted around, looking for an unseen death about to rip him open.

Behind him, Rosse rolled his eyes and yanked Cooper down hard by his pack.

"Get down, ya moron," growled Rosse.

Cooper turned to look at who or what had grabbed him, and came nose to nose with Rosse.

"Something you wanna say?"

Cooper nervously shook his head. "No."

Rosse ignored him, and turned his attention to scanning the area.

Cooper tried to slow his breathing when he saw his finger squeezing the trigger of his rifle; he would have sprayed the trees overhead if he hadn't forgotten to take the safety off first.

Forcing his hand to unclench his finger finally broke its grip from the trigger.

Satisfied nothing was approaching, Tate keyed up his mic. "Just a monkey," he said. "Let's move."

The squad stood up and headed out.

At the front of the line, Sergeant Wesson was picking her way through the growth, while keeping an eye on her compass heading.

She'd tied her bandana around her neck and had it pulled up, covering her nose and mouth to keep the bugs out.

Besides finding the best path to their checkpoint, she had to watch for other dangers; a dozing snake camouflaged as a vine or tree limb, a small dab of color could be a butterfly or a deadly poison dart frog. There were trees with two-inch spikes covering their trunk; the points of the thorns would go right through the thin leather gloves many of them wore, and the tips would break off deep in the flesh, causing certain infection if it wasn't dug out.

She had to see everything all at once, and was one of Tate's best people. Wesson was always strictly professional with Tate, and avoided parties when the group needed to get drunk and blow off steam.

She avoided giving anyone a reason to suspect Tate gave her special treatment, or worse, that they were involved; that wouldn't happen in her own team. Everyone in the squad either respected her as an equal, or feared her.

A few months after she started as Tate's operations assistant, she was having a beer with friends. At another table was a corporal, who had been competing with her for the posting. Still feeling bitter about it, the corporal had told his buddies that Wesson was screwing her way up the ladder, making sure the rest of the room heard him.

By the time the MPs arrived, she had beaten the corporal and his two friends to the floor. Witnesses in the bar said it was self-defense, and the corporal said he must have been too drunk to remember what happened.

The charges against Wesson were dropped. The corporal spent two more weeks in a cast, and the rest of his time at the base, avoiding Wesson like the plague.

The wind began to pick up, and brought dull, grey clouds that stretched across the sky. The horizon was dark grey, with heavy storm clouds coming their way.

Lightning flashed within the belly of the gloom, but the storm was too far off to hear thunder.

It felt like they'd been swimming in jungle for hours, when the tangle of green abruptly eased as the unit entered into sparser, younger growth.

To Tate, this signified they were very close to their checkpoint; any base would clear a wide perimeter outside its walls of anything offering concealment to the enemy.

This foliage looked about right for a couple years growth.

A moment later, the radio crackled in his ear. "Top," said Wesson. "We've made check point Phoenix."

7

DOGPILE

The team's approach brought them to the side of the abandoned DEA base. The compound was surrounded by double rows of chain-link fence, providing a patrol path between them. Each high fence was topped with razor wire. Observation towers stood in the four corners of the base, giving a clear view to the surrounding area.

Tate frowned as he assessed their position. With the fence in front and the jungle at their backs, they'd have a pretty bad day if the Vix came at them from the jungle.

Tate keyed up his mic. "Take up defensive positions. No noise."

Tate pulled the reconnaissance images from his combat vest pocket. He saw the main gate was to their left, a short distance away.

"Wesson and Ota," he said. "You two head left, and recon the main gate."

Each confirmed and quietly moved out.

Wesson was good as a tracker, but Kasey Ota was the best scout she'd ever seen.

People joked he could walk over potato chips without a sound. His blond hair, deep blue eyes and square features made him the poster-boy for a viking recruitment ad. He was friendly and enjoyed being around others, but hardly ever talked. While others were happy to share stories of their past, Ota was content to listen, and waved off questions about his past with a smile.

His past was a big unknown, except that somewhere along the line he became a devout follower of Zen philosophy. He didn't wear it on his sleeve, he lived it, and it unnerved the hell out of people who didn't know him, because no matter how dangerous or frenzied things got, he was as calm as a napping cat. It gave the false impression that he couldn't be relied on if things went bad, that he didn't take things seriously, or couldn't be counted on, but it was just the opposite; as the team's sniper, it gave him a deadly edge.

All the normal stress and anxiety other shooters had to deal with didn't exist in Ota's mind.

Ota and Wesson made their way around the corner of the perimeter fence, and after a few yards saw the front gate.

They checked the guardhouse and surrounding area of the camp through their binoculars, but saw no movement.

There was less jungle growth here, and it gave them a clear line of sight into the camp.

The gate was closed, and there didn't appear to be any signs of damage to any of the buildings. To their left, the camp bordered a river, but buildings and rows of large steel shipping containers blocked their view of the area.

"Top," said Wesson, keying her mic. "We're at the front gate. It's closed, but unlocked. No signs of movement."

"Copy that," replied Tate. "We're moving to your location."

Wesson and Ota scanned the area from the low brush as they waited for the rest of the team to join them.

Once there, Tate scanned the front gate and complex, but saw the same as Wesson and Ota; nothing.

He took out a satellite image of the base, and called the team together before their next move.

"Intel says there's no mines or traps in the area between the fences," said Tate, as he traced the perimeter of the base on the map with his finger. "The DEA report says they did an orderly bug-out and closed up shop behind them. It's likely local military stationed a small force here to secure the base for later use."

The Sergeant Major gave the base a quick glance, then returned to his satellite map. "There's no signs of the kinds of damage you'd normally see when Vix crash a party, so we may not have any contact, but don't get sloppy. If you see a closed door, leave it closed. We go through the gate and head to the boat dock. Monk, there's a boat house at the dock which should have what you need to get a boat up and running."

Monkhouse looked up from the map. "A boat engine sitting unused in the jungle heat and humidity for a couple of years? Should start right up," he said with a smile.

A brilliant flash of lightning snapped across the sky above their heads, followed by a crack of thunder that thudded in their chests.

"See?" said Monkhouse. "It just keeps getting better and better."

They could hear the beating of falling rain on the jungle a moment before it reached them. Warm water showered down, drenching them instantly.

"Once there," said Tate, "everyone else will set up a perimeter around the dock. Ota, see if you can't find your way up one of those watch towers and give us over watch."

Ota nodded, but said nothing.

"Okay," said Tate. "Wesson, you're with me. Everyone else, form up behind us, single file. From here on everyone observe radio SOP and keep chatter to a minimum."

The rest of the squad acknowledged, and prepared to move. Tate and Wesson went first, followed by Ota and the remaining team members.

Rain quickly turned the ground into mud, which sucked at their boots, but the road leading to the front gate was hard packed dirt and made the going easier.

Wesson did a quick check, and confirmed there was nobody in the guard booth next to the front gate.

The gate was latched, but not locked. It sat on a track that allowed it to roll to the side.

Tate scanned what he could see of the compound for movement or any signs of danger. The interior of the base sat on packed soil, and except for isolated patches of weeds there was little opportunity for jungle growth to take over.

"Rosse and Fulton," said Tate, pointing to the two men. "Open the gate, and do a quick recon. The rest of the team will keep watch."

At the gate, Rosse looked at the compound, seeing nothing more than he did before.

"Two years in the Army, and all I get to open is a damn gate," said Rosse, as he spit out his gum.

"I hear ya," said Fulton. Picked fresh from the load of recruits from boot camp, Specialist Jeff Fulton was one of the new guys to the squad.

Tate saw potential in him, and had chosen him for the team; putting him in with more seasoned soldiers would speed up his training. Paring him up with Rosse would toughen him up. The veterans in the team didn't like 'baby sitting', and wouldn't cut new guys much slack, but if noobs kept their mouth shut and eyes open, they could learn a lot from the guys with field experience.

Rosse looked at Fulton like he'd just shot out of a cow's ass. "What do you mean, you hear me?"

"You know," said Fulton, realizing he'd just said the wrong thing. "Like, I know what you mean."

"How would a green scrub know what I mean, Specialist?" asked Rosse, looking at Fulton like he had just spat on Rosse's mother.

"No, Sergeant. I mean, I understand...," said Fulton. "Uh... no. I don't know what you mean."

"You're damn right you don't know," said Rosse. "And you keep on not knowing until I say otherwise. Now open that gate, and don't talk to me unless you got something to say that don't sound like a donkey farting."

Fulton pulled on the gate, which only moved a few inches, then stopped. He pulled harder, but it didn't move.

Rosse gave him a withering stare, and Fulton quickly went to work, yanking on the gate until it started to move with a rusty squeal.

He pulled the gate open a few feet, painfully aware of all the noise he was making, but hoped it would be masked by the heavy downpour.

Rosse brushed past him, muttering, "Stupid kids, acting like they know jack all." He did a quick scan of the compound for movement, but saw nothing and moved deeper into the camp.

There were three, steel cargo containers to the left of the main dirt road that lead further into the camp. To his right, there was a building with a couple of large roll up doors, probably a garage.

Rosse pointed to Fulton, and then to a couple of buildings ahead to the right.

Even though he was drenched from the rain, Fulton looked like he was sweating bullets, not sure if he was more afraid of Rosse or the Vix, but Rosse was there and the Vix weren't, so he moved up to scout the buildings.

He checked the doors, finding them locked, and then looked in the windows. He signaled back to Rosse that there was nothing.

They continued through the rest of the camp, not finding any signs of recent activity or Vix.

"Yeah, boss," Reported Rosse, over his radio to Tate. "I got nothing here. Come on in."

The team joined up with Rosse and Fulton in the center of the compound.

Tate took out his map and orientated the team to their surroundings.

"The west perimeter fence parallels the river. That fence has a gate that opens up to a dock where our two patrol boats are supposed to be tied up. I don't expect any Vix activity, but I want Ota and Twigg to stand watch at the dock entrance. Monkhouse, you'll check out the condition of the boats. Everyone else can find a place out of the rain until we're ready to go."

Tate put the map away and looked around his squad. "Questions?"

Nobody answered, and Tate headed for the dock gate, with the squad following.

A few minutes later, the squad came around the corner of a building and saw the dock gate.

Like the front gate, this one wasn't locked, or secured either. Tate thought it was strange that the compound hadn't been locked up, or ransacked. It was possible that scavengers had never found this place, but with it being on a river it seemed likely that somebody would have noticed the place.

He didn't have an answer, and turned his attention to the here and now.

Their intel was holding solid. Nobody else seemed to notice, but to Tate it was a small miracle.

Back when he was part of the 471st intel, it was critical to their missions. The world wasn't static; it kept on changing and it was a given that the intel they got was outdated before it landed on their briefing desk.

After joining Mortuary Affairs, his squad never needed anything more than just a drop point and a direction.

'Walk around and shoot anything that's not human' was the typical directive.

Tate had to smile, because just as the intel described, there were two boats tied up at the dock. Both were rigid-hull fast boats, with twin diesel turbocharged motors. An inflatable collar of tough Kevlar and polyvinyl ringed the hull, giving the boat greater buoyancy and allowing it to stay afloat, even if the boat took on water.

Monkhouse was standing next to Tate, sizing up the tasks ahead of him. The boat on the right side of the dock was down-river of the current, and debris had piled up around, making it look like the boat was sitting in a birds nest. The protective tarp tied over its awning was in tatters, and the hull was partially filled with green scummy water.

The boat on the left side of the dock was in much better condition, partly from being protected by the dock. The tarp over the awing was weathered, but in good condition; at least it wasn't listing to one side like its counterpart.

"Looks like you have your hands full," said Tate, with a wry smile.

"Maybe it's not so bad," said Monkhouse with a shrug. "How much time do I have to get them usable?"

"You're the engineer. How much do you need?"

"Well, the batteries are probably flat. The fuel's gonna have condensation, so I'll need to drain and refill the system, and check for cracks in any hoses. Fix any leaks in the collars..."

"I get it," said Tate, taking the hint. "How long?"

Monkhouse absentmindedly scratched a bug bite on his arm. "Maybe six hours."

Tate said nothing, but stared at him.

"Or five," said Monkhouse. "I could do five. Is five okay?"

Tate stared at him, unblinking.

"Four," said Monkhouse. "Bare minimum. Anything less and I promise you that tub will break down before we get halfway there."

"You have two," said Tate. "Grab who you need to help. If they're not ready by then, we strip the boat down to the hull and row. I'd hate to be the one to tell the squad you're the reason they have to paddle to our objective."

"Two hours? I thought *I* was the engineer."

"You are," smiled Tate. "And I'm the guy in charge of the engineer."

"You know, you're letting this sergeant major rank go to your head," said Monkhouse good-naturedly, as he walked down the dock and disappeared under the tarp of the left boat.

A short while later, the rain trailed off, until it stopped entirely.

Monkhouse had assessed the condition of both boats, and was handing out assignments to squad members.

Tate was going over the landmarks they'd use to plot their course to the ambassador's villa and back, when Monkhouse gave him a report on the boats.

"The right boat is a mess," said the engineer. "With a lot more time I could get it working, but I can get the left one running in less than an hour. Between the two boats, I think I can rig up working parts."

"Good to hear," said Tate. "It'll be nice to get out of the jungle onto the open water. I can't remember the last time I felt fresh wind in my face."

"We were in a helicopter, like just a few hours ago," said Monkhouse. "Wasn't that windy enough?"

"I wonder if the local Vix have ever tasted Monkhouse," said Tate. "What do you think?"

Monkhouse took the threat in his stride, but got the message. "I think I hear someone calling my name. Lovely chatting with you, but I have to go."

Monkhouse returned to the usable boat, where Rosse was taking the filter off the fuel line.

He showed it to Monkhouse, who examined it with disappointment.

"Look at this thing," said Rosse. "It's shot. Them billion dollar satellites didn't tell us about that."

Monkhouse frowned as the filter seeped black gunk over his hand. He tossed it back to Rosse, hoping it would splatter him with the sludge, but it didn't.

He grabbed the rag hanging from Rosse's belt and wiped off his hand. "Do you need a billion dollar satellite to tell you to grab the filter off the junked boat?"

"That *is* the one from the junk boat, smart guy."

"I really treasure these little moments with you," said Monkhouse, as he tucked the mucky rag in Rosse's pocket. He walked over to Sergeant Wesson, and explained his dilemma. "I need your help finding another filter. Maybe it's in storage. If you can't find that, then I'll settle for solvent. Maybe we can wash the thing, maybe not."

Wesson called over Private Cooper, and they set off in search for a storehouse or work shop.

The compound had been designed to handle up to thirty permanent personnel, and everything needed to sustain them for six months. While the admin building and barracks didn't require much space, the support facilities, DFAC, garage, medic station, and storage made up nearly seventy percent of the compound's size.

Wesson and Cooper's search took them near the back of the compound, where they found the headquarters and barracks. The doors were locked, and since it wasn't likely boat parts would be stored in either, they left them alone.

Looking through the grimy window, Cooper saw a row of bunks with footlockers at the end of each. The side table nearest the window had a small picture propped up against a windup clock. A woman and small boy smiled out of the photo, cheek to cheek. A blue toy dinosaur stood next to the picture.

It was an unwanted reminder of the day the sirens abruptly came to life in Cooper's small town. National Guard trucks roared onto their street, and soldiers pounded their fists on everyone's doors. The defenses had been overrun.

Get out now, or we'll leave you. Everything he had disappeared as the truck turned the corner, and his home was gone from sight.

They came around the back of a long building, which they discovered was the DFAC. Further up, they could see across the compound to the gate leading to the boat dock, but a building blocked their view of the dock and the people working on the boats.

The only thing Wesson and Cooper hadn't checked out was the row of steel cargo containers next to the DFAC building. Eight of them sat in a row, some green, a couple red and a blue one. There didn't appear to be any order to them, with nothing on the doors to say what was inside.

Cooper unlatched the thick steel handle on the first one. The door groaned on the hinges as he strained to open it.

Beyond the limited reach of the sun, the interior of the container was darkness. He groped over the flashlight clipped to his combat vest, looking for the on switch.

It only took a moment to snap on the light, but in that moment Cooper's mind had filled the darkness with rotted, clawing hands reaching out for him.

The beam of light banished his imagined fears, leaving him looking at stacks of boxes. He went inside and started pulling them out.

Wesson went to a red container next to Cooper's, and shoved up on the latch to get it to move.

As she heaved the door open, a wave of putrid stench rolled out of the container. Adrenaline shot through her body, and she jumped back as she grabbed the pistol grip on her LM-948 and leveled it at the darkness within the container, with her finger squeezing the trigger.

Nothing happened; no sound or movement came from inside it.

With a shaking hand, she reached across her chest and turned on her flashlight. The beam revealed only boxes and a couple of large broken jars that had exploded from the prolonged heat. Greasy ooze had run down the jars and puddled into a disgusting mound of yellow and green mould.

Wesson took a breath and let go of her death grip on her machine gun. She looked around, fearing someone had seen her acting like an idiot, but her few seconds of fear passed completely unnoticed.

Wesson shouted over to Cooper, louder than she wanted. "Hey, Cooper. When you're done with that container, I got another one here for you."

Cooper's voice dully echoed from the other container. "Yeah, okay."

Wesson went to the third container and pushed up on the latch. She was mildly surprised how easy the latch was to move, when the steel door slammed into her.

Seeing stars, she stumbled backwards and tripped over her own feet, falling hard on the ground with a grunt.

Blurry figures sputtered and growled as they came into the light. The world came into horrifying sharpness as a pack of Vix shambled near her, staring up into the sun.

After nothing but darkness, the sun was the strongest sensory input to them, but Wesson knew she only had a few seconds before they turned on her.

She looked for her gun, which had fallen a few feet away. To get it she'd have to move and certainly draw the Vix's attention.

But it didn't matter, because one of the Vix tripped over her foot and fell on her. Small slivers of rotted flesh fell off when it smacked into her.

Instantly, the thing started chewing on Wesson, clawing and ripping at her.

Luckily, it was attacking her combat vest, but the Vix would shred though that protection quickly.

An involuntary scream blew out of her lungs as she tried to fight the thing off, which instantly galvanized the team.

When Cooper came around the container door, it took a moment to process what he was seeing. A few of the things were standing looking left and right, trying to zero in on where the sound of food was coming from.

Four of them were on the ground, digging at something, and that's when he saw Wesson's arm flailing from under the pile.

He ran straight for her arm. As he reached her, one of the Vix on top of her looked up at him, growling.

Without slowing down, he kicked the thing in the face, shattering its head into fragments of bone and ooze.

Adrenaline was pounding through him, and when he grabbed Wesson's arm he yanked her so violently that he pulled her clear of the mound of thrashing corpses.

Wesson was beating at the empty air, locked in the grips of panic.

Now all of the Vix were fixed on the both of them and coming.

Cooper let go of Wesson and went for his rifle. It wasn't there; he'd left it leaning inside the container.

He looked up, just as the nearest one reached for him. He kicked the thing in the chest, knocking it back, but lost his footing in the muddy ground and fell next to Wesson.

As Cooper struggled to get up, his hand fell on something hard. Looking down he could see the shadows of the undead throng, nearly on top of him.

Under his hand was Wesson's LM-948. He didn't think about chambering a round, or checking if the safety was on. He just squeezed the trigger.

Bursts of flame strobed as Cooper poured an endless salvo of machine gun fire into the converging Vix.

Chunks and limbs flew off, as wads of supersonic lead cut through them, until there was nothing left but a pile of wrecked pieces.

He and Wesson were littered in empty shell casings, as smoke hissed out of the glowing red barrel of the gun. It had only been seconds, but the terror still gripped him. Cooper's ears were ringing and he didn't realize he was screaming until he ran out of breath.

A scream echoed around the compound, making it hard to tell the direction it came from.

Tate brought up his rifle. Quickly scanning his surroundings, he took a head count.

"Where's Wesson and Cooper?"

Monkhouse shook his head. "Somewhere in the camp."

Tate fought down the panic trying to hammer out of his chest. "Rosse, Fulton, Ota, go left. Everyone else with me!"

They began to fan out when a long burst of gunfire ripped the air, stopping everyone where they stood.

Tate identified the direction of the sound and charged towards it.

The others hesitated a moment then chased after him.

Tate rounded a building, catching sight of the carnage, but all he saw was Cooper next to a mound of bodies.

"WESSON!" A splinter of horror shot through him.

An instant later, he saw Wesson on the other side of Cooper.

"Someone get Cooper," Tate yelled over his shoulder. He skidded around Cooper and dropped to his knees next to Wesson.

The rest of the team arrived a second later, and ran over to Cooper.

"You're okay. You're okay," chanted Tate, but it sounded more like pleading than a promise.

She looked up at him as he tore to get her combat vest off.

"Monkhouse, check her arms and legs."

Monkhouse immediately went to work, checking Wesson for wounds.

"How's Cooper?" shouted Tate.

"Checking," yelled Rosse, kneeling over Cooper.

His eyes were fixed straight ahead, and he didn't seem aware of Rosse next to him.

Rosse tried to take the machine gun from Cooper, but his hands had a death grip on it. Rosse put a gentle hand on Cooper's arm and gave him a reassuring squeeze.

Cooper broke his gaze and faced Rosse, recognizing him with mild surprise.

Rosse gave him a friendly smile as he eased the gun from Cooper's grasp. "It's okay, tough guy. You got 'em."

8

THE VILLA

Cooper vacantly looked at the pile of meat scraps he'd created as Rosse and Ota lifted him to his feet, before examining him for wounds. A solid pat on the shoulder from Rosse snapped him out of his daze.

"He's pretty rattled, boss, but he's okay. No bites."

Monkhouse gave Tate a nod that Wesson was okay, too.

Tate got her combat vest off and flipped it over, relieved to see the Vix hadn't clawed through it.

Tate scooped her up in his arms and squeezed her to his chest. "I'm here, now. I'm here," he whispered to her.

"Uh, they top?" said Monkhouse, gently. "Maybe she'd feel better if we got her away from all this."

Tate looked around at the bodies and nodded in understanding. "Yeah. Take them back to the boat dock. Give them some water and something to eat if they can manage it."

They helped Wesson to her feet and walked both of them over to the boat dock, while Tate and Ota stayed behind.

Together they walked around the cargo container, then came back to the pile of destroyed Vix.

Tate forced himself to refocus his mind. He'd almost lost Wesson, but that was then. This was now.

"You notice something wrong here?" said Tate.

Ota nodded in agreement.

Tate looked at the inside of the container door. "It's not like they locked themselves in the container to hide. There's no way to latch the container door from inside."

"They still got a lot of meat on the bone," said Ota. "I don't think they've been dead very long."

Tate looked at Ota with surprise. "Are we looking at the same thing?"

"These guys are stewed," said Ota, "not rotted. Put meat in a sweltering steel box and let it simmer in its own juices..."

"Yeah, okay," said Tate. "I get it. What else have you got?"

Ota took out his K-bar knife and picked through the scraps of undead remains, and lifted up a ripped sleeve of camo pattern shirt. Sewed onto the shoulder was a round patch, with an eagle holding two daggers. Written in the border around the patch was 'Brigada Fuerzas Especiales'.

Ota rummaged through the remains, finding more clothing. All of it appeared to be from uniforms.

"What the hell are Colombian special forces doing in a cargo box?" Tate thought aloud.

Ota stopped his gruesome probing and grinned at Tate. "You're gonna love this," said Ota.

Judging by Oats grin, Tate knew he wouldn't. He knelt down next to him and looked at what Ota was tapping with the tip of his knife.

Tate picked up the shattered remains of an arm with a broken wristwatch. He slid the watch off and wiped away most of the reddish-black organic sludge.

It was a cheap Rolex knock-off, with chronograph display and oversized bezel that tried too hard to look rugged and tactical.

What caught Tate's attention was that the watch had been broken two days ago.

Just then, Monkhouse walked up, looking over their shoulders. "Good news, Top. I got one of the boats working. We can leave when you're ready. Hey, nice watch. Can I have it?"

The twin, in-line six cylinder turbocharged engines pushed the boat through the water at forty knots without cracking a sweat.

A couple of times one of the engines coughed, belching out black smoke, but Monkhouse said it was just buildup and nothing to worry about.

Tate barely noticed as he puzzled over the bodies in the cargo box with Wesson and Ota.

"The pieces of uniform on the Vix weren't new, but they were clean, and one scrap had a crease from being freshly ironed. At face value, those men had been alive a day ago, two at the outside."

Sergeant Wesson was recovering quickly from her near death, and the fresh sea spray helped clear her thoughts.

"So, not only were those Columbian special forces guys in that DEA camp, someone else was there and killed the Columbians."

"Busy place," said Ota.

Tate furrowed his brow as he thought through the details of the camp. "Whoever it was went to a lot of trouble to cover their tracks. There weren't any shell casings."

"And if there were any boot prints, the rain would have washed them away," added Wesson.

"My bet is even if it didn't rain we wouldn't have seen anything," said Tate. "And that leaves the thing that's bothering me the most."

Ota turned his face into the wind and smiled as it whipped through his hair. "You're wondering why they put all the effort into making it look like nobody was there. Why not hide the bodies in the jungle?"

Tate's expression went from thoughtful to troubled, as his gaze turned to the passing coastline. "I think someone killed those men and left them in that container, knowing they'd turn. I think it was a trap."

Wesson followed Tate's stare and looked at the lush foliage crowding the coast, imagining hidden eyes watching them and feeling very exposed out in the open.

"Someone knows our mission."

"Yes, they do," said Tate.

The sun was a couple of hours from its zenith, as the boat rounded a small point of land and brought their objective into view.

A simple dock extended from a beach of cream-colored sand that rose up to the front of an impressive Spanish-style house.

A large flag-stone patio opened onto the beach. Behind it, the grand two-story house overlooked the entire cove from glass walls that spanned the entire front of both floors. A balcony jutted out from the second floor on the right end of the house, with a decorative black wrought iron banister.

Attached on the left end of the house was a high turret, covered in river rock; its arched windows overlooked the beach and patio.

Rosse pulled the boat onto the dock, and Private Fulton scrambled out of the boat and tied it off.

The cove was protected from the large swells of the ocean, and the boat rode easily with the gentile surf.

Tate and Wesson scanned the building from the boat with their binoculars, while the rest of the team waited.

"No signs of movement," said Tate.

"How do you want to do this?" asked Wesson.

Tate put away his binos and looked at the building thoughtfully. "Normally I'd throw a noise maker and draw out any Vix. Be easy enough to take the boat out and shoot them from a distance, but...," Tate rubbed the stubble on his jaw. "I got a funny feeling about this mission. I think we need to do this quietly."

The team moved up the beach to the patio in a loose line, two abreast.

Tate felt good about the extra training they'd had, but it wasn't enough. He was encouraged to see them being alert for any movement and keeping good spacing between each other, but then Fulton swept the aim of his gun across the backs of three team members in front of him.

Tate had to grind his teeth to bury his frustration. He made a mental note that when they got back to base, Fulton was going to pull so many hours of weapons safety he'd forget what his barracks looked like.

It was another reminder that even with the best in his team they were only good enough; he could trust their desire to protect their team, but they didn't have the experience or skills for him to trust their competence. Just the opposite, his old special ops team of Night Devils were a tight woven unit that thought, moved, and fought as one. Each man was an individual warrior, yet part of a collective force.

The absence of that bond ached like the phantom pain of a lost limb. Tate caught himself spiraling into the guilt and remorse and snapped his mind back to the present, just as they reached the patio.

Still a grand house, it wore the haggard look of being long abandoned. Weeds pushed through the gaps in the patio paving stones, and the outdoor furniture was bleached and torn. A couple of windows had broken panes of glass, but were otherwise intact and closed.

As the team moved across the patio, they saw two sets of glass French doors leading inside, which were also closed; a good indication the place didn't hold any Vix, but not good enough to drop their guard.

Ota checked the door, which was unlocked. The hinges rasped as he pushed open the door into a large living room. Daylight flooded through the windows and glass doors, making it easy for Ota to see his surroundings.

Leather furniture circled a large fireplace on the right, and a teak bar and four barstools were on the left. At the other end of the living room, an open stairway circled up to the next floor, and next to that was a hallway leading deeper into the house.

The air was stale and smelled of dirt and dust, but didn't have the sickly stench of rotting flesh. Nothing was knocked over, or out of place. There weren't any dried ooze footprints, or any other signs of Vix.

Keeping his weapon up, Ota keyed his mic with his free hand. "Place looks empty."

"Everyone, inside," said Tate over the radio. "We're going upstairs."

Ota started up the stairs until his eyes were level with the next floor, where the stairs emptied onto a broad landing, which opened to several rooms. Light beige walls rose up to a wide skylight that covered the entire landing.

Just like below, the second floor showed no signs of undead. He started up the stairs again with the team following.

The second floor landing was easily large enough for the entire team.

Tate divided them up to check the rooms, and each of them reported back no contact. From their intel, Tate knew the safe was located in the office to his right. There wasn't any sign of Vix, but Tate wasn't going to risk getting cornered by surprise if they showed up.

"Rosse, you take up a position in the turret room at the right end of the house, and Fulton, you're on the balcony on the left. Ota, scout the rear of the property. Check any out-buildings, paths, roads. Wesson, you have watch at the top of the stairs."

Before Tate got to him, Cooper spoke up. "I can stay with Sergeant Monkhouse and help with whatever he needs."

Tate looked at Monkhouse, who shrugged his shoulders. "Yeah, I suppose I might need him."

Cooper still didn't know how he would get the documents once the safe was open, but this put him closer to that possibility, as long as he was able to fight the reckless desperation that was gnawing at him to grab the files and run the first chance he got.

A wall of large windows gave the office a stunning view of the cove and the turquoise sea stretching into the horizon. The sun had bleached the wood floor and furniture, but even weathered it was impressive. A stout wood desk commanded one end of the room, while four leather chairs sat around a marble table at the other end.

Tate crossed the room to the wall behind the desk, covered by a thick tapestry.

Behind the desk was a large tapestry depicting two Spanish knights fighting on horseback. Around them, a surging tide of foot soldiers were locked in endless silent battle.

Tate pulled back the thick tapestry to reveal the door of a wall safe. Electricity was a thing of the past for this house, making the keypad useless.

Tate had memorized the combination to both the keypad and

wheel lock, but wasn't surprised when it didn't unlock the safe; in his experience, people changed the combination of their safes all the time.

"Monkhouse, it's time to work on those black arts of yours. Remember, we want what's inside to stay in one piece."

Monkhouse unslung his combat pack with a wounded look. "I'm hurt that you have so little confidence in me."

Tate watched Monkhouse dig his tools out of his combat pack and lay them out on the floor.

"How many safes have you cracked?"

"Like this one?" said Monkhouse, as he tested the cordless drill. "Probably never."

A disturbing realization crept over Tate. "How many other types of safes?"

The safe and his tools seemed to be the only thing that Monkhouse would look at; he wouldn't make eye contact with Tate.

"I don't know if they'd qualify as a traditional safe, but they had locks."

It took all of Tate's willpower not to throw Monkhouse around the room until he'd exhausted himself. "We're out here because you said you could open this. Now you're telling me you can't? I should abort this mission and leave you here."

"I never said I couldn't open it," said Monkhouse. "I just didn't say I had never cracked a safe. This is our fist mission. If you'd turned it down because we couldn't open this thing, do you think they'd give us another? None of us want to be out there pulling crap patrols. This was our one shot at getting away from that, and I wasn't going to let it get away from us. I can open it."

Tate held him in an angry stare.

"I can!"

"We're out of here in twenty minutes," growled Tate. "That was the original time you needed, and that's what you'll get."

"Sledge," snapped Monkhouse to Cooper, who fished out a hammer-sized sledgehammer and quickly handed it to him.

Monkhouse swung and knocked a big chunk out of the wall. "I'll have it open, Top."

Tate walked the first floor of the house to cool off. He understood why Monkhouse had bent the truth, and maybe, if he were a different man, he would have done the same. But he wasn't a different man...

Tate caught himself in that thought. He was different. Different from every one of the soldiers in his battalion. They were civilians in uniform, playing soldier; everyone from convicted criminals to accountants were deemed qualified to do the grunt work of reclaiming the new South America. Hump a backpack and shoot straight enough to kill a Vix was all you needed in order to qualify.

Tate could feel that familiar depression pooling around him. He was a warrior, highly trained and part of an elite esprit de corps, but he'd never know that feeling again; to be part of something that made a difference.

Instead, he was mired in inadequacy. His team tried hard, and Tate believed their training had made them a step above the others, but it wasn't nearly good enough.

His thoughts were broken as something heavy thudded to the floor above him. He went upstairs and into the office, to see a gaping hole where the wall safe had been. A bundle of wires snaked out of the hole and into the back of the safe, where it laid amongst the debris.

Tate watched as Monkhouse stripped the insulation from several of the wires, then cracked the housing for his cordless drill battery.

In spite of their earlier fight, Monkhouse was pleased to see Tate. "Perfect timing." He tied the end of a piece of wire to two wires leading to the safe.

Then, using a pair of pliers, he stuck the other end of the wire into the drill battery. The electronic keypad on the safe blinked, then went off.

Monkhouse hummed to himself as a puff of smoke came out of the back of the safe. He took the wire out of the battery, then spliced another piece of wire to a different set leading to the safe.

Tate's curiosity won over his anger. "What are you doing?"

Monkhouse held the new piece of wire with his pliers. "I'm glad you asked. A standard safe works off a wheel lock with tumblers, proven to be very effective against thieves, but not very fancy. Then one day, a marketing genius came up with the idea that they could make the boring old safe sexy and modern by slapping some electronics on them. Great for sales, bad for security. The tumblers in this safe only need gravity to work, but the computer needs electricity, which can be unstable. Like, what to do in the event of a power surge. If the internal motherboard ever got hit with a power surge, it would lose its database of things like alarm settings and oh, I don't know, combinations to open the lock. So, they programmed it to reset the combination to the factory default."

Monkhouse put the other end of the wire he was holding into the drill battery. The keyboard panel on the safe blinked a few times then stayed lit.

"And that's why you shouldn't always trust 'new and improved'." Monkhouse pressed zero on the safe keypad four times.

He turned the handle on the safe door and opened it.

Fulton had been keeping watch from the balcony that overlooked the patio all the way to the beach.

The rhythmic waves lapping up on the surf had a hypnotic effect, and he could feel his eyelids getting heavy. His eyes drooped closed, and he could feel himself drifting off when he heard a thud from the office down the hall.

He opened his eyes and caught the fleeting image of a figure disappearing into the thick foliage to his left, bordering the patio below.

He reached for his radio to report it, but stopped to question that move. Had he really seen something, or was it a trick of his mind? He didn't want to admit he'd been dozing, and took his hand away from the radio.

He stepped back from the balcony and out of the sunlight, but was still able to keep most of his vantage point.

From the ground, the glare off the exterior walls made it impossible to see into the darkness that Fulton had stepped into.

Standing in the cooler shade, Fulton could hear Tate and Monkhouse talking when his radio crackled on.

"This is Tate. We'll be done shortly. Be ready to move out."

Tate's update was welcome news. Fulton was hungry and lethargic from standing in the sun.

The dock was blocked from his view by trees and shrubs but he could see the cove, and thought how good it would be to be back in the cool spray of the ocean.

His thoughts were broken by a wisp of black smoke climbing upwards. He brought up his rifle and looked though the four power scope, and saw it was coming from the direction of the dock.

As he reached for his radio, he saw movement from the same shrubs, as before, and a figure stepped out. This time there was no doubt in his mind. It was very real.

In the time it took for him to bring up his rifle, he saw the figure was dressed in dark mottled clothing and wore something bulky around its chest, but none of that registered; his overriding thought was to take down the Vix ASAP.

As he squeezed the trigger, the Vix lobbed something like a black can out of its hand.

Fulton snapped off two quick shots, hitting the Vix perfectly in the chest and head.

As it fell, Fulton heard the breaking of glass as the black can went though the French doors below.

Suddenly there was a flash of light from below and a deafening explosion.

Fulton's radio came alive with people shouting, but he was too bewildered to make sense of any of it.

He looked back at the Vix he'd just dropped, and gaped as it came back to its feet.

Dazed from the explosion, he dully watched as a rifle appeared in the Vix's hands, aiming it at the balcony.

Suddenly, several figures swept out of the bushes around the patio.

Over the ringing in his ears, Fulton could hear a peculiar *pop, pop, pop*, and bits of the walls seemed to be crumbling.

He squeezed his radio. "Hey guys... I think the boat is on fire."

Suddenly something kicked him in the chest like a battering ram, and blood sprayed his face.

Stumbling back, his feet tangled beneath him and he fell onto his back. His lungs refused to breathe and the room seemed too dark.

Gasping, he wiped at his eyes, and his fingers came away wet. As he tried to blink his own blood out of his eyes, the room swirled away into darkness.

9

FIRE FIGHT

Rosse's radio crackled to life.

"This is Tate. We'll be done shortly. Be ready to move out."

He was getting tired of standing around. He'd been keeping an eye out for Vix from the second floor of the turret attached to the house, but since they hadn't seen any by now he was sure there weren't any around.

Of the two windows in his room, he was gazing out over the distant side of the property, which ended abruptly at the jungle. He had his back to the window that looked out onto the patio.

He flinched as he heard two cracks of a rifle from behind him.

Rosse had enough time to see there was a body laying on the patio when there was a sudden flash of light, and every pane of glass in the downstairs blew out.

It was a moment of disbelief as several figures emerged from the shrubs, dashing for the house. They were all wearing combat rigs and carried machine guns.

Adding to the surrealism, the body laying on the patio picked himself up, knelt into a crouch and started spraying bullets at Fulton's balcony.

The danger to one of his own snapped Rosse into action. "Oh, the hell you are!"

Furious, and scared for Fulton, Rosse brought up his HK 556L and squeezed the trigger of the under-barrel grenade launcher. Nothing happened.

"Damn it!" Rosse fumbled with the safety and pulled the trigger again. The rifle punched his shoulder as the grenade shot through the window, exploding near the crouched shooter.

Metal shards lashed out from the grenade, throwing the shooter across a lounge chair; he didn't get back up again.

The shrapnel fanned out in every direction, wounding three more intruders and bringing them to the ground.

"We're getting attacked," Rosse shouted into his radio. "They're coming inside, and they got guns!"

Posted at the top of the stairs, Wesson turned her attention down the hall as she heard two shots come from Fulton's direction.

An instant later, there was a searing white flash and concussion blast from the floor below.

Her ears were ringing, but she could hear Rosse yelling a warning from her radio. Dazed, she looked down the stairway and saw two faces looking up at her.

There was a strange moment where everything seemed to stop as they made eye contact.

They wore dark green and brown mottled fatigues under black combat vests. Their helmets were painted in the same camo. Their guns were unfamiliar, but looked sleek, deadly, and were pointed at her.

Her head cleared enough to see the danger, and she moved back from the stairway just as they opened fire. A stream of bullets chewed up the wall next to her as they walked their fire in her direction.

The skylight exploded in a shower of glittering rain. She cursed as she felt bits of glass fall under her shirt collar and down her back.

She stuck her machine gun over the railing, trying not to expose herself to their guns, and hosed the stairway with return fire.

She caught a blur of movement as Rosse ran past her and down the hallway.

Tate and Monkhouse came into the hallway, nearly colliding with Rosse.

"Armed bad guys. I think Fulton's hit," said Rosse, and ran down the hall towards the balcony room.

Things were happening fast, and Tate was worried. People were shouting over each other on the radio.

Wesson was shooting in near panic mode, burning through her ammo.

His team hadn't trained for combat, let alone a full on firefight.

Confusion was everywhere, and Tate knew his team was on the edge of disintegrating into chaos.

"Everyone shut up," he snarled over the radio, and was rewarded with instant quiet.

"Rosse, check on Fulton. Ota, I need an update as soon as you have something. Wesson, short bursts. I'm sending you support." He knew he was stating the obvious, but everyone else's head was clouded to it. "Monkhouse, you're with Wesson. I'm getting eyes on the enemy. Listen for me on the radio, got it?"

Monkhouse gaped like a fish out of water. "With Wesson... doing what?" he asked.

Gunfire rattled down the hall where Rosse had gone. Tate had to get there quick.

"Support Wesson. Keep anyone from coming up the stairs, and get me eyes on the enemy," said Tate, then took off after Rosse, leaving Monkhouse dazed and worried.

"Since when do we have an enemy?"

Tate came into the balcony room, finding Rosse kneeling next to Fulton who was laying on the floor, his chest and face splattered with blood.

The private saw the sergeant major standing over him, looking concerned. "It's oh shit thirty, right Top?"

"Yes, it is," said Tate, and knelt down to help Rosse.

Broad and squat, Rosse was built like a tree trunk. An ex prison guard, his rough edges had rough edges, but he was a natural medic. His large meaty hands worked deftly as he examined Fulton's face and neck for wounds.

"Where's it hurt?" he asked.

"Hard to breathe," said Fulton.

"Check his chest for..." started Rosse, but Tate already knew what to do and had slid his hand under Fulton's chest plate, pressing his fingers, probing for holes.

"Ahhhhh, that hurts," snapped Fulton.

"I know," said Tate. "But the good news is you don't have any serious wounds." Rosse nodded in agreement.

"Nothing serious?" said Fulton. "I'm bleeding everywhere!"

"Easy kid," said Rosse. "It's your arm that's bleeding. You're gonna be okay. I'm gonna get you..."

Something came through the balcony door and clattered across the floor behind them.

"Grenade," yelled Tate. He dove at the grenade, grabbing it then flinging it back outside.

Just as it disappeared below the edge of the balcony, their ears were hammered by the explosion.

"Flash-bang," shouted Tate over the ringing in his ears. "Come on," he said to Rosse.

They grabbed Fulton by his combat vest and dragged him into the hallway.

He patted Rosse on the shoulder to get his attention. "Give me a sitrep."

Rosse crunched his eyebrows together, recalling what he had seen. "Six, maybe seven guys, all wearing the same stuff, loaded for war. Looked like them movies with the Special Forces guys."

Tate quickly put together the situation and what had to happen next. "Can you handle Fulton?" he asked.

Rosse nodded.

"Good," said Tate. "Listen for me on the radio and be ready to move." Tate gave Rosse a reassuring smile and headed down the hallway.

It took a moment for Cooper to realize he had been left alone in the office, and scattered at his feet were the documents he craved.

One moment Cooper was watching his only chance to save his

family disappear as Tate was stuffing the documents into a small bag, then there was an explosion and all hell broke loose.

Tate dropped the bag and ran out of the room with Monkhouse. Some of the documents had spilled out, and Cooper knew if he was going to make his move it had to be now.

He grabbed a handful of documents, but stopped as his mind groped where to hide them. The longer he stood there, the faster it felt like time was speeding up.

Exposed, fear and panic immobilized him. Any moment now, Tate would catch him in the act.

"Cooper, what the hell are you doing?" Tate stood framed in the doorway, holding a smoking machine gun, looking like an instrument of death.

His face was streaked with sweat and blood, and Cooper knew the last thing he'd see would be a bright flash as Tate splattered him across the wall.

"Get your shit together and help Rosse," yelled Tate. "We're pulling out of here." And then he was gone.

A moment later, Rosse came into the room with Fulton and sat him against a wall, as Cooper, stunned, only stood and watched.

His second of indecision had saved him. A moment later and Tate would have caught him stealing those pages. Tate would have seen him for the traitor he was and killed him on the spot.

"The hell's wrong with you, Cooper? Ya look like ya seen a ghost." Not waiting for an answer, Rosse started working on Fulton, cutting his sleeve open to the shoulder.

Fulton's arm was thickly sheathed in blood. It was too much for Cooper, and the room began to swim before his eyes; everything was going dark.

Rosse's voice slapped into Cooper's consciousness like a jagged icicle, snapping his world into focus.

"COOPER, you dickhead! Get over here and help."

Cooper dropped the documents and rushed over, kneeling next to Fulton, hoping he didn't vomit on him.

Rosse tore open a packet and took out a wad of gauze. Cleaning away the blood made his arm look less like a horror movie, and revealed three bullet holes that began seeping blood again.

He dug into his kit and pulled out a bag, tore it open and poured white powder on Fulton's wounds. Grabbing a roll of bandage, he tossed it to Cooper.

"Take this. Wrap it tight around the wounds on his arm, but don't cut off circulation, got it?"

Cooper nodded, still trying to comprehend what was happening. "Today, Cooper," shouted Rosse.

Cooper started wrapping the roll of white bandage around Fulton's arm. If he was feeling any pain, he wasn't showing it.

"What about his face?" asked Cooper. "Is he going to die?"

Rosse smirked. "Nah, he ain't gonna die. His face is fine. Finish what you're doing and bring 'him into the hall." Rosse closed his medic pack and ran out of the room.

The gunfire outside was interrupted as Cooper heard two loud pops, then someone on the radio yelled, "Tear gas!"

Cooper quickly tied off the bandage and tried hauling Fulton to his feet.

Fulton drunkenly tried to get up, but was mostly dead weight and too heavy for Cooper.

Tate ran down the hallway to the turret room, where Rosse had been at the start of the attack. Careful he didn't draw attention, he peeked around the edge of the window, where he could see down onto the patio and partially into the living room.

One of the attackers was draped over a patio chair, and he could just make out two figures at the base of the stairs, aiming their weapons at the second floor.

Another figure stepped out onto the patio, giving Tate his first good look at their enemy.

He wore a dark mottled uniform with integrated knees and elbow protective pads. His jump helmet was wired with a radio that connected to an assault vest fat with spare magazines.

These guys weren't Americans, but they were special forces of some nationality.

Tate didn't see any others, but guessed they were somewhere inside.

The soldier opened a pouch strapped to his leg, and took out a canister. He pulled out the pin and took aim at the window above him.

Tate snapped his HK 93 to his shoulder and hit the solider center mass. The bullets impacted with a distinctive thud that Tate instantly recognized as body armor.

The soldier went down with a grunt, dropping the canister, which began spewing thick white gas.

Caught in the cloud, the soldier started gagging and scrambled to his feet.

Tate shot him again, this time aiming higher, tearing away half his neck.

The soldier fumbled to stop the gout of blood from the fist-sized chunk missing from his neck, then fell forward, dead before he hit the ground.

The window frame exploded as bullets ripped into the turret window, but Tate was already gone. He'd seen enough to piece together what was happening, and knew his team would be slaughtered if they didn't bug out right now.

Turning the corner to the landing, he pointed at Monkhouse.

"You're with me." He keyed up his radio. "Ota, tell me you got something."

"Yes," said Ota. "Far end of the property."

"Great," said Tate. "We're heading your way. Out." Tate came into the office, with Monkhouse close behind.

Cooper was struggling to get Fulton up, and Tate grabbed Fulton's combat vest and easily lifted him to his feet. He turned his attention to snatching up the documents from the safe, and shoved them into his combat pack.

After a last look to check he hadn't missed anything, he grabbed his radio. "This is Tate. We're bugging out. Wesson will cover the stairway. Rosse, join up with Cooper and get Fulton down the back hallway. Meet up with Ota at the back of the property. Once you're outside, stay quiet. We don't want these guys to know where we are. Move like you have a purpose. Tate, out."

Propping Fulton up, Cooper quickly left the office, leaving Tate and Monkhouse.

Wisps of CS gas began snaking into the office, and Tate knew they were running out of time.

Tate had been sizing up the situation, and realized if they were going to escape he'd have to delay the op for long enough for the team to break contact and call in the extraction.

The trick was creating a distraction big enough to keep all of the hostiles busy, so they wouldn't see the team withdrawing.

"You have any explosives left?" asked Tate.

Monkhouse took a black package the size of a thick book out of his pack. "I didn't think we'd need much, but this is what I got."

The CS gas began burning at the back of their throats, as Tate directed Monkhouse to the hole in the wall where the safe had been.

"Put it there and set the timer for one minute."

Monkhouse held up a small box with a red button on it. "Timers? Where are we, in the stone age? Just say when." He dropped the explosive into the hole in the wall.

Monkhouse looked a little confused as Tate took the detonator.

"We're done here," said Tate, and ran into the hallway with Monkhouse close behind.

The hallway was thick with the bitter, pungent taste of CS gas. Tate's eyes were streaming and he could feel his lungs burning, but his combat experience had taught him how to dig deep and push through it.

Wisps of gas swirled around Wesson as she doggedly held her ground. Tears and snot ran down her face as the gas relentlessly punished her senses.

Tate patted her firmly on her shoulder. "Good job, Sergeant. It's time for you to go. Join up with Ota and withdraw out the back. Go about a klick and call in the helo."

"Like hell, Top," said Monkhouse. "We're not leaving you."

"Jack! Sergeant Major," said Wesson, catching herself. "No way I'm going without you."

It had been a long time since anyone had put themselves in harm's way for him. In that moment, he felt a bond with the two people who stood resolutely in front of him. The unexpected emotion seemed to fill him with renewed strength.

"Go. Now. That's an order. Just don't shoot me by mistake when I catch up," he said with a grin.

Wesson and Monkhouse nodded, then headed down the hall. Tate watched them go, then turned his focus to the stairway.

Blinking through his runny eyes, he saw shadows moving below, near the stairs.

A quick glance behind him showed the hallway was clear. His team was out.

He stepped back from the stairwell. "Pull back to the office with the safe," he shouted. "We'll hold 'em off there."

He aimed down the stairs, waiting for them to take the bait.

A few seconds later, two dark figures appeared on the stairs.

Tate made a mental note that, whoever they were, they understood English.

Tate lit up the stairway as he fired two short bursts down on them, then instantly dodged away. Gunfire spouted from the ground floor, tearing up the floor and surrounding walls.

Tate took off after his team, just as a someone threw a flash-bang up the stairway, which clattered across the second floor landing.

The other end of the hallway opened to a wide loft, and Tate was almost there when the grenade went off. The corridor funneled the concussive blast directly at him, just as he ducked around the corner, missing the head splitting force by the skin of his teeth.

The concussion blew out the floor to ceiling windows, spewing glass across the lawn.

To his left, open stairs curved to the floor below, which emptied into a broad, grassy field, bordered by a high wall. Tall trees crowded the other side of the wall where manicured lawns ended and the jungle began. When the time was right, that would be his way out.

Wesson and Monkhouse joined up with the rest of the team, waiting on the other side of the wall.

They looked battered and exhausted, but Wesson knew they weren't safe; not by a long shot. At best, they'd only bought themselves a few minutes. She couldn't let their fatigue take hold, or she'd never get them on their feet.

"Everyone on me. Cooper, you're our comms now."

Cooper was already wearing the radio pack he'd taken from Fulton when they were patching him up in the office.

"Check your weapons and load fresh magazines."

Rosse had Fulton's rifle and his own slung across his broad barrel chest, looking like a human pillbox. "That's what I'm talking about. I want another chance at those pricks."

"Not today," said Wesson. "Orders are to withdraw and extract outta here."

"What happened to Top?" asked Rosse.

Wesson slung her gun over her shoulder. "He'll catch up. Let's go, and remember, fast. I want everyone to stay quiet." Without another word she headed into the jungle.

No sooner had the flash-bang gone off, Tate heard boots pounding up the stairs.

As they passed by the hallway, he counted off the seconds, visualizing the enemy stacking at the office door then charging inside.

They'd know they'd been tricked the instant they saw it was empty. He flicked the cover off the detonator switch and pressed the button.

A crack of thunder and light slammed into him, throwing him off the landing. He cart wheeled through the air, inwardly cringing at the imminent crunch of bone when he hit the imported Italian marble floor below.

Something reached out of the smoke and dust and punched him across the body, smashing the air out of his lungs and stopping his fall.

The smoke cleared enough for him to see he'd landed across the downstairs couch. Wheezing for air, he rolled off the back and tucked himself behind it.

If he saw Monkhouse again, he'd never let him off the hook for nearly killing him. The smoke was thinning as Tate heard boots running across the landing above and down the stairs.

Five shadows emerged though the smoke, silhouetted against the light from the backyard.

"They're gone," growled one of them. "The only way out is through the yard. We'll search the house in case they dropped it. You three find them and take them out."

One of the men hesitated. "Dex, our orders were no deadly force."

"Now you got new orders," said Dex, as he racked the slide on his gun. "Am I clear? Good. I'll send you back-up to help search. Move out."

From what he just heard, Tate guessed there was another squad positioned at the dock as a reserve force.

Three of the shadows headed into the yard.

Tate knew they'd quickly find the breach in the wall his team had used. The other two went back upstairs.

His first move was to stop the leader from calling in reinforcements. A stabbing pain shot through his side as Tate pulled himself off the floor; he was sure at least two ribs were broken. It would slow him down, but it wouldn't stop him. Fighting the pain, Tate climbed the stairs after the two remaining men. He'd just started down the hallway when he heard the crackle of a radio.

He recognized the voice of their leader from downstairs.

"Five men," said Dex. "You need to move fast, so only water and weapons."

Damn it! Too fat, too slow, thought Tate; he couldn't hold off that many men. He had to get out... right after taking off the head of the snake.

He slid up to the corner of the hallway and called out, "Dex, we got 'em."

Surprise was written across Dex's face as Tate came around the corner with is rifle up, instantly putting two rounds into his head.

The second man's reactions couldn't save his life. In the same breath Tate killed Dex, he blew out the back of the other man's head with two quick shots.

Before the dead body hit the floor, Tate was on the back stairs, heading for the breach in the wall.

The adrenalin of the firefight had long burned off, and the team were working hard to keep pace with Wesson.

Luckily, they'd found a game trail, making the going easier. Beneath the ever-present canopy, the jungle floor rose and fell in a series of low rolling hills, dotted with a light undergrowth of ferns and palms, but as they moved deeper inland the jungle thickened.

Tendrils of vines spider-webbed between trees, and tall ferns masked roots that tangled and tripped the careless.

Wesson changed directions a few times to throw off any pursuers, and a moment before had Monkhouse set a booby-trap for added punishment; her gut told her the enemy wasn't far away.

Before she'd completed that thought, the booby-trap exploded. *They're right behind us!*

"Everyone take cover!"

The team scattered for the nearest fallen tree or rock, and the jungle came alive as heavy gunfire sprayed into their position.

Bullets chewed off chunks of wood and chipped stone as Wesson and her team squeezed themselves into the dirt.

Wesson had landed in a shallow depression behind a rotted log. She had to do something to interrupt the enemy's fire long enough so they could shoot back.

She propped her gun on the log, while staying out of sight and blind fired at her best guess of where they were.

Instantly her log was hammered with incoming rounds.

"Rosse, grenade!"

Rosse was in cover behind a dirt mound when he heard Wesson call him. He rolled onto his back and unslung his HK 556L. He tugged open the pocket on his combat vest, and grenade shells spilled out over his chest onto the ground.

Bullets ripped the air inches above him as others smacked into the mound, spraying dirt into his eyes and mouth.

"Son of a... shit!" Rosse groped the dirt near his side as he blinked the soil out of his eyes.

Confusion filled him as he saw a blurry figure appear above him.

His vision cleared and he froze in terror as he saw a Vix standing over him. Its clothing was black with grime and hung in shredded rags. Most of its shirt was gone, exposing sickly, wet skin peeled back from a huge hole in its side.

Rosse could see a swarm of shiny black beetles crawling under moldy green ribs, and fought against the vomit surging from his gut.

Inexplicably, the jungle went eerily quiet as the shooting abruptly ended. An instant later, a scream tore the air.

———

Tate grimaced against the scything pain of his broken ribs, as he followed the tracks of the three men hunting his team.

Heat, sweat, and thirst were pushed from this thoughts. His only goal was to catch these men. The trail led him out of the shadows of the canopy and onto a wide, rocky flat.

Puffing hard, he ran to the distant edge of rock. Desperately, Tate scanned for anything that would give him a direction. It was taking too long; he was hemorrhaging time.

His head snapped up at the sound of an explosion. The sharp crack of gunfire opened up nearby, and he bolted towards it.

Tate came to a stop beside a cluster of dense brush. The sounds of assault rifles were coming right from the other side of it, interspersed with the chatter of a machine gun farther away.

He guessed at least one person on his team was shooting back, until a couple of rounds punched through the foliage inches from his head, then all doubt was removed.

"This is Tate," he whispered into his radio. "I'm down range from your location. Everyone hold your fire. I say again, do not shoot."

The last thing he needed was to be shot by his own team. The distant machine gun went quiet, and he cautiously peered through the foliage.

From his vantage point, Tate was directly behind one of the enemy soldiers. Out of the corner of his eye, Tate saw movement through the gaps between the palm leaves several feet to his left.

That's two of them, Tate thought, but where's the third? He feared the missing man was flanking his team, but which way?

There wasn't time to find him. Tate knew somewhere behind him another enemy pursuit team was closing the distance.

He pulled his Ka-Bar clear of its sheath and moved smoothly through the brush.

In one practiced motion, he grabbed the soldier and drove the knife into the base of his skull. His gasp of surprise died in his lungs.

Tate pushed the body away and snatched up the dead man's rifle. The second soldier glanced up in alarm as Tate came through the palm leaves, shooting as he moved. He dropped the soldier quickly with a three round burst.

Now he had to find the... Dirt and wood spat up as bullets chewed the ground, inches from Tate. Forty feet away, the third man broke cover.

Tate snapped the borrowed rifle to his shoulder and fired. The rifle kicked only once, telling Tate the magazine empty.

At the same time, the other man stopped shooting, his gun empty, too.

The men hesitated in the abrupt silence, watching each other.

Tate broke the stillness, dropping the empty rifle and reached for his own, slung from his shoulder. With deftness of motion, the other man hit the mag release with one hand, while grabbing a fresh magazine with the other. It was a race of seconds who would be shooting first.

It happened so fast neither man saw it coming.

Tate was lifting his rifle to his shoulder as the other chambered a round in his gun.

Two Vix broke from the dense green behind the soldier, who let out a gut wrenching scream as they fell on him with a snarl.

They attacked with a frenzy, clawing whatever was in reach. The man grunted, trying to push himself up as one blindly gouged at his backpack, ripping away shreds of fabric with its teeth. The other tore into the back of his leg, burying its face in the raw, wet muscle and blood.

He let out wail of pain, fixing Tate with his gaze, beseeching him for salvation.

Tate nodded imperceptibly and fixed him in his gun sights. He snapped two quick rounds and the man's face dropped into the dirt, free from his suffering.

The gunshots did nothing to distract the Vix from their hunger, making them easy targets for Tate. One after the other, he shot them in the head and their motionless husks slumped over the dead soldier.

"Squad, this is Tate," he said into his radio. "All hostiles are down. I'm coming over."

Tate flinched as a gunshot cracked to his right. He pivoted, looking for a target but saw nothing.

The next thing he heard was Rosse yelling somewhere nearby.

"Son of a bitch, puss bucket, ass cracker," bellowed Rosse. "Get this shit sack offa me!"

Tate ran to the source of all the yelling and found Rosse scrambling to get out from under a motionless Vix.

Wesson was grinning down at him with a satisfied expression. "You know, most people have the decency to get a room."

Rosse untangled himself and flung the corpse off. He jumped to his feet, brushing away real and imagined beetles.

"Yeah, really funny."

10

ESCAPE

It had been an hour since Tate had rejoined the team. Hoping to outdistance the second pursuit team, he pushed his squad at a demanding pace, but in his gut he knew they'd never make it back to the checkpoint before the enemy caught up.

Alone, he could easily evade his trackers and make it back to Checkpoint Phoenix, but he'd have to cut his team loose, condemning them to a death sentence at the hands of their attackers.

Tate remembered two missions with the Night Devils where he faced the real possibility he'd have to die for the success of the mission; luck or providence had intervened, and he had lived to see another day.

The experience had taught him that sometimes lives had to be sacrificed for the mission to succeed.

Looking at the sweat-streaked faces of his team, he weighed his next decision; theirs wouldn't be the first faces he'd committed to memory, but were those secret documents worth six lives? Somebody thought they were, enough to violate a UN treaty, invade US soil, and risk starting a war.

But, *this* wasn't war and, Tate decided, those rules didn't apply here. In fact, because the secrecy of the mission was already compromised, a lot of rules about this mission had been swept off the table.

Tate made his decision. Everyone was getting home today.

"Cooper, bring me the radio."

Everyone watched as Cooper brought it over and powered it up.

Tate set the frequency reserved for the mission and made the call. "This is Rover Actual. I say again, this is Rover Actual. Requesting hot extraction. Over."

Tate released the transmit button, waiting for a reply, but the radio only hissed uninterrupted.

It was nearly a minute before the radio crackled as a voice replied. "We copy request for hot extraction. Rover Actual, authenticate."

Tate keyed the mic. "This is Rover Actual. Authentication is Romeo, Oscar, five, five, niner. How copy?"

"Copy, Rover Actual. Chopper is airborne and heading to your extraction point."

"Exfil location has changed," said Tate. "New location is grid four, three, November..." He was interrupted by a loud burst of static, followed by a different voice.

"Negative, Rover Actual," said the new voice. "You're exfil location cannot be changed. Mission secrecy it top priority."

Tate didn't know who this was, but he could smell arm chair generals a mile away. "This is Rover Actual. Authenticate." He released the transmit button and waited.

The radio hissed and nothing more.

"I say again. Authenticate. Who is this?"

The hiss was broken as the unknown voice replied. "Return to your designated extraction point for extraction."

Tate bit back his flaring anger. Memories of calls for help while critical seconds ticked by, only to be given incompetent orders by some Powerpoint Ranger comfortably sitting behind a desk miles from the danger, flashed to his mind.

"Negative! We have wounded and are pursued by hostiles. We need exfil right now."

Tate glared at the radio, daring it to speak, but it only hissed.

He tried to reach the helicopter, but whoever had cut into his transmission was jamming his radio.

"What's that mean, boss?" asked Rosse.

The muffled sound of one of Monkhouse's booby-traps boomed somewhere in the distance.

"It means we move out," said Tate.

Tate had taken point, and was moving at a pace he knew was pushing the limits of his team.

Knowing she'd keep everyone moving, he set Wesson to bring up the rear. They'd been going hard and the jungle fought back just as hard, sucking their energy, grabbing at anything it could sang, clutching clothing and gear to slow them down.

Behind him, someone vomited, and Tate knew it wouldn't be long before his people started dropping from heat exhaustion. It was either that or stop and fight... and probably die.

Trying to evade their pursuers wasn't working, and Tate decided it was time for a new plan. He came to a stop and the rest of the team halted in their tracks.

Momentum had been the only thing keeping them on their feet, and the moment they stopped most of them sagged to the ground, not caring where they sat.

Tate met up with Wesson to explain what he was planning. Her uniform was torn and filthy, and her face and arms were criss-crossed with dozens of fine cuts.

He figured he didn't look much different.

"Hell, Sergeant, you look like someone locked you in a sweat box with a pack of pissed off wildcats and rolled it down a mountain."

A smile cracked Wesson's stoic expression. "It was only a small mountain," she said, then got back to business. "They don't have much left," she said, nodding towards the rest of the team.

"We'll give them a few minutes to hydrate and then figure out our next move," said Tate, but he already knew there was nothing to figure out; they weren't going anywhere, and Wesson knew it, too.

She looked at the jungle around her, half expecting to see their attackers emerge from the shadows. "Do you think they're still after us?"

The team had heard Wesson, and Tate knew they were listening for his answer. Someone else might have chosen false comfort of a lie over grim honesty, but that wasn't Tate.

As exhausted as they were, they'd buy into a lie if it meant they didn't have to move anymore. If there was any chance of survival, Tate needed everything the squad had left; he wouldn't get that with a lie.

"You can count on it." Someone in the squad groaned. "I'm going to check out the surrounding area," said Tate. "Everyone stay quiet. Back in a few."

Within ten meters, the team was lost to his view. Tate was looking for an area best suited for an ambush. He wasn't afraid of a fight, even a losing one, but if it came to that he wanted every possible advantage.

He was making his way through the dense brush when he heard voices and froze. He slowly crouched, merging with the surrounding light and shadow. His thumb eased against the safety on his rifle, turning it to off, as he continued to listen.

He quickly realized these weren't the operators hunting them. He only heard two voices, and there was a casual tone about them.

The voices began to fade as they moved off.

Staying in the cover of the jungle, Tate quietly tracked them.

Soon he heard the unmistakable sound of flowing water; a lot of it.

The voices had stopped moving, and he crept up to a break in the foliage to see what was happening.

Two men were leaning against a tree by the bank of a narrow river.

Their clothes were dirty and worn. One wore a sweat-stained, faded orange baseball cap, the other a straw cowboy hat with holes in it.

A short distance from them was a pile of large burlap sacks, heaped up on a creaky-looking dock.

Judging by the two neglected AK-668's propped against the sacks, neither man seemed concerned about security.

There could only be one reason these men were out here, and Tate was sure it was because those sacks had coca leaves in them; it looked like the cocaine business wasn't going to be slowed down by something as minor as the near extinction of the human race.

Tate wasn't interested in these two men, or their coca leaves.

What had his full attention was the boat tied up at the end of the dock.

After Tate discovered where these men were going he'd get his team; it looked like they were taking a boat, after all.

After a few minutes, the two laborers left the dock; following a worn path, they disappeared out of view.

Half a mile away was their pickup truck with the last of the harvested coca leaves. Transporting the leaves from the field to the field lab was boring work, but as they were regularly reminded by their pendejo boss, if they didn't like the job they could try their luck avoiding the undead and reach civilization.

Following the fin del mundo, the Cartel lost its hold of the cocaine business and all out war broke out among the smaller drug bosses. It was a blood bath of drug lord wannabes, all grasping for as much territory as they could get.

Things began to settle down after most of the challengers had been killed off; eventually, only a handful of rivals were left.

Battered and depleted of forces, they settled for peace, agreeing to split up the territory in equal amounts.

None of this mattered to the two laborers. They'd been doing this for fifteen years. Bosses came and went, but the job was always the same, until today.

Each of them were glad to lay the last of their haul with the rest of the burlap sacks. Now they could take a break before loading up the boat and delivering them to the processing lab.

Neither of them noticed their rifles were missing until a man emerged from the bushes with a weapon pointed at them.

Tate looked over the sights of his rifle at the two men, whose expressions were almost comical. He guessed they were so relieved he wasn't a land-shark they didn't mind having a gun pointed at them.

"Ingles?" asked Tate.

Both nodded. "Si," said the one with the ball cap.

"Good," said Tate. "What's your names?"

"Mateo," said the one wearing the ball cap, pointing to himself, then pointed to the other man. "Hector."

"Nice to meet you. Good news and bad news, guys. The good news is I'm not going to kill you. The bad news is I'm taking your boat," said Tate. "Sergeant Wesson, get everyone loaded up."

The rest of the squad came out of the jungle and loaded into the boat, while Tate kept his eyes on the two men.

"Where's your radio?" The cartel didn't care if anything happened to these two men, but it cared a lot about anything that threatened their business, so they made sure communications were readily available to everyone.

"It's in our truck," said Mateo.

"Here's what's going to happen," said Tate. "Do exactly what I say, you live. If you don't..."

Tate nodded to Wesson, who brought up her machine gun.

Both men's eyes went wide with fear.

"You two are going to head back to your truck and then use your radio to let me know you're there. I want to hear both of your voices. Once you do that, we'll leave."

With Wesson aiming at both men, Tate handed Mateo a scrap of paper. "Here's my radio frequency."

"Okay, no problem," said Mateo, quick to be as agreeable as he could; the sooner they didn't have guns pointed at them the better he'd like it. "There's extra gas in a can."

"Everyone load up in the boat," said Tate.

Wesson and Cooper pushed the boat into the water, and the squad quickly got in, followed by Tate, who kept his eyes on the two Columbians.

He saw the gas can and gave it a shake, satisfied by its heft and the sound of sloshing inside.

"All right guys," said Tate to the two laborers. "Time for you to go. Don't forget, I'll be waiting to hear from you on the radio. Don't make me come looking for you."

The two men backed away with all the caution of withdrawing from a coiled viper, not wanting to make any sudden movement that could get them shot.

Hector broke first, turning and running out of view, with Mateo following close behind.

Tate started the engine and pushed the throttle half way up. The boat looked like junk, but the engine was strong and responsive.

They'd gone a couple hundred yards up-river when his radio crackled and came alive with somebody franticly chattering in Spanish.

"Luis, this is Mateo. A bunch of American soldiers just took our boat. They got lots of guns. If you hurry you can catch them. Bring everyone! Let's kill those assholes."

Tate pushed the throttle all the way up, and the boat quickly picked up speed. He couldn't help but smile as he keyed up his radio.

"Mateo, is that you?" There was a long pause, then a very anxious Mateo answered.

"Uh... si?"

"In all the confusion I forgot to tell you one of my people found your truck. I thought in all the excitement you might forget you were supposed to radio me, so they switched your radio frequency for you."

This wasn't Tate's first rodeo; he knew these guys would turn on him at the first chance they got.

He needed time to put as much distance between him and the Columbians as he could, and keeping them off balance would buy him valuable time.

"If I see Luis I'll be sure to tell him how helpful you've been to me."

"No, no, no," stammered Mateo. "I'm sorry. I have a family. They'll kill all of us."

"Put Hector on," said Tate.

"Hello?" said Hector.

Tate was satisfied that neither man had stayed behind to watch which direction he'd taken the boat.

"Listen very carefully to me, because there's two very important things you need to know, all right?"

All he got in response was a very worried, "Si."

"The first thing is I left your guns in the bushes behind the sacks of coca leaves."

"You left the guns?" asked Hector.

Tate could hear Hector repeat what he said to Mateo.

"Why would you do that?"

"Because of the second very important thing. There's a group of very pissed off soldiers coming your way," said Tate.

"More Americans?" asked Hector, with renewed worry.

"No, not Americans," said Tate. "We got reports someone is killing off the drug lords and taking over their operations. We were on patrol when we got ambushed by them. They're coming for your boss, so you should probably call for more men."

"Si! I mean yes," said Hector. "Uh... thank you for the warning, señor."

"Good luck, guys." Tate put down his radio and caught Wesson looking at him with a mixture of concern and confusion.

"What is it, Sergeant?"

"Those guys after us aren't interested in drug lords. They want the intel we took from the villa."

Tate smiled at her. "They lie. I lie."

Using his map, Tate navigated the several tributaries that branched off from the river to their exfil without incident.

If Mateo and Hector took his warning seriously regarding the incoming soldiers, there'd be an entire cartel militia waiting for them. He doubted any of those operators would survive that, but he wouldn't lose any sleep over it.

His only regret was not being able to capture and question one of those guys; he had a lot of questions that would go unanswered.

While the rest of the squad ate or slept during the helicopter ride back to their base, Tate tightened down the bolts on his boiling anger, because whoever put this mission together was either a full-fledged idiot, or leaked the mission.

Either way, Tate would find out, but for now he needed a clear head to think through everything that had happened on their mission, and if the combined pieces told a bigger story.

It was shortly after oh two hundred when the helicopter was wheels down in the base, and the crew chief shook Tate awake.

Tate's body protested with every move as he climbed out of the Black Hawk. He felt like he'd been trampled in a stampede.

The squad shuffled into formation, waiting for his final instructions.

Tate thought if he looked half as bad as them, he must be a damn wreck.

"Debrief..." said Tate, then paused to check his watch, realizing he had lost track of time. "Uh... thirteen hundred hours. Someone help Rosse get Fulton to medical. Dismissed."

The squad started to break up when Tate stopped them. "I'm proud of you. All of you. We were thrown into something you weren't trained for, and you overcame the challenge. It could have gone a lot worse. Good job."

Alone with his thoughts, Tate entered his quarters and dumped his gear on the floor. He turned on the shower, adjusting the knobs until the water was as hot as he could stand it.

Stripping off his ACUs was a slow and painful process.

Blood from cuts all over his body had dried to his clothing, and he winced in pain as he peeled them off, opening some of the wounds in the process.

He stepped into the shower and spasmed involuntarily, as the hot water bit into every cut, scrape and bruise. The pain faded quickly, while the water rinsed away the grime.

The heat and steam soothed his aches and eased his fatigue. His mind circled back on the details of the mission, refreshing his determination to get answers out of Colonel Hewett.

Nearly two weeks had passed since Tate had sent the Colonel the mission packet containing the documents from the ambassador's villa through a secure courier, and Tate hadn't heard a word back from the colonel.

The times he had called, his assistant had said the Colonel was 'away', politely taking Tate's message.

Tate didn't like being in the dark, and it was beginning to feel like colonel was dodging him. His suspicions of Hewett's involvement grew by the day.

Tate had vented his growing apprehension through strenuous exercise; each day demanding more of himself, hoping that exhaustion would be a cure.

In the end, he had to admit that all he was getting out of it was blisters, near heat exhaustion, and dehydration.

His memories roamed of their own volition to the life he used to have with his comrades from the Night Devils. There was only so much stress, fear and anxiety a warrior could squeeze into that little box each man kept inside himself. The tensile strength of courage allowed them to persist in each mission, in the face of all the instruments of death their enemy confronted them with. But after a while, the seams of that Pandora's box would start to come apart, and it was time for the Night Devils to decompress, loudly, vigorously and usually at the expense of property damage in a bar, and bail from a local jail. But that was another time, and the brothers that knew him almost as well as they knew themselves had been abandoned because of his own failings.

Before his memories and self judgment sucked Tate down into that familiar emotional black abyss, he headed into the city and surrounded himself with people.

Twenty minutes later, Tate was standing under the vibrant glow of the Blue Orchid's neon sign.

Rocko's massive frame stood by the club's entrance, giving the impression he had never moved from the last time Tate was there.

There were several people lined up to get inside, and Tate paused as he decided if he was in the mood to stand around, or find another place to go when he heard Rocko's voice rumble next to him.

"No need to stand out here, Mr. Jack. The boss says he's always got room for you."

As Tate followed Rocko to the front door, he glanced up at the awning that stretched over the steps leading to the entrance, and spotted the reflection of a camera tucked in the shadows.

Teddy, the owner of the club, came across as scattered and preoccupied, but Tate suspected he was more clever than he led people to believe.

As he passed the doorman, he made a point to look at Rocko when he turned his head, and saw a flesh-colored earpiece.

Tate guessed that whoever was monitoring the cameras updated Moon on who was outside. Moon was probably giving Rocko instructions via that wireless earpiece. It made being watched feel like customer service.

Tate thought of all the times he'd shown up and never once considered he was being watched. It was a small thing, but he chided himself for not catching the cameras sooner. *You're losing your edge, bub. Been too long since you've done real spec ops*, thought Tate.

Inside, the sounds of a normal packed house washed around Tate as he walked up to the pretty hostess. A live band was playing Artie Shaw, as a willowy woman in a sequined dress sang Deep Purple, just over the sound of the low buzz of people talking.

The hostess guided Tate past his usual place at the bar to a booth in the back of the club. Tate would happily trade Teddy's VIP treatment for a stool at the bar, where he could keep the time between having his drink refilled down to a bare minimum.

Someone was reading his mind, because a waitress appeared at his table with a tumbler of bourbon.

Halfway into his second bourbon, Tate was feeling the teeth-grinding tension of the past couple of weeks defusing into a relaxing fog.

He was far from drunk, but the alcohol was softly garroting his troubles to death. He knew they'd be resurrected tomorrow, but for now, mission completed.

"Jaaaack. How did you sneak in here without me knowing?" said Teddy. His blond hair was almost as shiny as the sequined dress of the singers. He was wearing a muted navy herringbone suit, with a tropical dress shirt of tiny fish and a broad tie.

"How is everything? Is the staff taking good care of you?"

"Just fine, Teddy, uh Commodore," said Tate, correcting himself before Teddy could.

To Tate's surprise, Teddy sat down in the booth and looked at him over his steepled fingers for a few moments.

If it wasn't for the bourbon, Tate would have lost patience being stared at. Instead, he was slightly amused and a little uncomfortable that Teddy might be hitting on him.

He was very wrong on all counts. "Jack, as you know I'm a man of discretion."

"I didn't know that about you."

"It's very high on my list, especially when it comes to my customers. That's why when someone came here asking about you, I didn't say a word."

Teddy had his attention now. "What did they want to know?"

A waitress came over and put a drink down in front of Teddy. "Anything else, Mr. Moon?"

"Thanks, Angel. We won't need anything for a while," said Teddy, flashing her a big smile.

He turned his attention back to Tate, ignoring the drink. "He didn't want to say too much, but said he had a business proposal for you. Something about your trip out to the ambassador's villa."

Tate was stunned. How was information about a classified mission getting into the hands of a nightclub owner?

"That's a classified mission. If you know something about a leak you need to tell me."

"Keep your shirt on, Jack. Anything I know about your mission I heard from the fella asking for you. He's very interested in talking to you. He said you stole one of his boss's boats."

It took a moment for Tate to make the connection. It must be the boat they'd taken from the two drug workers back in the jungle.

This wasn't making sense. How would they know who took their boat, or where to find him? If he wanted any answers, he'd have to meet this guy.

"Let him know I'll be back here tomorrow night. We can meet then."

"I'll make the arrangements, Jack," said Teddy.

11

A DEAL WITH THE DEVIL

The following night, Jack walked into the Blue Orchid and was silently escorted to a private booth.

Seated at the table was a well-groomed man, who was occupied with a small notebook. His suit had an expensive and tailored look to it. Several of his fingers wore tastefully crafted gold rings that stood out against his deep brown skin.

Tate sat down across from him without a word. He had few cards to play in this game until he knew what was going on; better to let the other guy do all the talking.

A waitress put a bourbon in front of him, which he thanked her for.

The man closed his notebook and slipped it inside his jacket. He looked at Tate with a pleasant smile and extended his hand across the table.

"You are Sergeant Major Jack Tate, yes?" He spoke with a minor Spanish accent that was more an embellishment than a sign of his native language.

Tate shook his hand, expecting it to be soft, but instead it was the firm, calloused hand of someone who didn't spend his life behind a desk.

"Yes, that's me," said Tate.

"Sergeant Major, I'll get to the point. I understand you've been operating in Valle del Cauca, where you took a boat belonging to my employer."

It wasn't lost on Tate that this man hadn't introduced himself or explained who he worked for; he sensed this stranger was measuring him up.

Was Tate a simple soldier who had stumbled across a drug lord's operation, or had it been a planned mission to identify and wipe his business out?

Could he be intimidated by a man in an expensive suit, confused how this stranger knew he'd been to the ambassador's villa? Or anxious that a complete stranger had tracked him down, knew his name and maybe knew a lot more?

This stranger had a game plan, and Tate knew the quickest way to the short end of the stick was to play by someone else's rules.

It was time to introduce some new rules.

To the stranger's surprise, Tate stood up to leave. "I'm sorry. It looks like you went to a lot of trouble to find me, but I don't have your boat anymore. Thanks for the drink, but I'm gonna have it at the bar."

The stranger hurriedly came out of his seat, leaving behind some of his suave composure in the process. "We have one of the soldiers," the stranger blurted.

Now he had Tate's interest. He sat down again, trying very hard not to give away how hungry he was to get his hands on this soldier.

"And you're here to trade this soldier for something I have?" asked Tate.

After the initial ruffling, the stranger recomposed himself. "Not the soldier, exactly. We're interested in a trade of information. We provide you a window of opportunity to acquire whatever information you can from him, and in return you provide us information useful to our needs."

"From where I sit, you already have more information than I do. Why don't you balance things a bit by telling me who I'm talking to, and who you're asking me to get involved with?"

"I'm encouraged my proposal hasn't frightened you away. Since we've gotten this far, it's only fair, as you say, to balance things. I am Dante Barrios. I am the advisor to Nesto San Roman. He is the head of a minor industry, part of which you came across during your recent mission. Your forewarning of the approaching soldiers gave us enough time to prepare for them. Only one survived, but one is enough."

Barrios absently clinked his rings lightly on the glass of his drink, creating space for Tate to make the next move.

Tate put the pieces together quickly. Roman was running a coke operation in Columbia. Just like everywhere else, the outbreak must have wreaked havoc on the cartel. The survivors must have all charged into the vacuum of power to take what piece of the operation they could get away with. Occasionally, the warring drug bosses slaughtered each other in power plays to expand their operations and take out the competition.

San Roman must have seen a way to give his fiefdom an edge through a deal with Tate.

"What kind of information does the soldier have that I'd want?"

Barrios' smile took on a forced quality, and he seemed less comfortable than a moment before.

Whatever deal Barrios was proposing, Tate suspected he'd just found a hole in Dante's plan.

"San Roman does not have an interest in the squabbles of other countries. He will allow you one day's access to this soldier. You can question him for yourself."

Tate took a measured sip of his drink as he let Barrios' words sink in. When it clicked into place, he laughed out loud.

"He won't talk, will he? You guys tortured him for information, but my guess is he's some country's special forces. The kind of extreme resistance training he's had made your interrogation look like amateur hour, and that's why you're here. You're thinking if I can get him to talk, and that's a big 'if', I'd be willing to cut a deal with you guys? Mr Barrios, it sounds like I'm doing all the work in this proposal of yours."

"I will say that our conversations with him were less productive than we expected. But, you see, I think it's doubtful you will experience the same reluctance with him. The reason I'm here is because he asked for you. By name."

Tate's instincts were tingling. Who was this soldier? Who sent him, and how did he know about Tate? More importantly, what else did he know?

He had to be careful with Barrios. Getting into a *business* deal with even a small time drug boss could make Tate's life badly complicated, fast. Was the risk worth the reward? It always came down to that.

"Did he say anything else?"

Dante Burrios smiled. Whatever he was about to say, he felt like it would seal the deal, and that made Tate nervous.

"Yes," said Dante. "He seemed to feel it would be of significant interest to you. He said, 'good is the enemy of great'. Did I say that right?"

Tate's mind fumbled with those words, trying to attach them to something that was naggingly familiar. His thoughts groped through fragments of memories for the connection.

Suddenly, the realization slammed home, leaving him rocking between disbelief and anger; those were the words he'd spoken to Private Cooper.

Sergeant Wesson had commented that Cooper had been on his phone the morning of their mission. When they were attacked at the villa, Tate remembered finding Cooper with a handful of those secret documents.

Cooper was a mole, and his treachery had nearly cost everyone's lives; there was no question in Tate's mind that he would do just about anything to get the rest of the information from Dante's prisoner.

"What does your boss want in return?"

"Forewarning, nothing more," said Dante. "You will contact us regarding any planned encroachment of your military into San Roman's territory."

"*His* territory? You understand that the entire South American continent is now part of the United States?" said Tate.

Dante Barrios sat back in his seat, gazing around the club with an expression of boredom. "Sergeant Major, geo-politics holds no interest for me. Let's return to the reason I'm here. We give you information, and you do the same for us. Do we have an agreement?"

"And if your boss gets a heads-up US soldiers are going to be in his neighborhood, what's he going to do to them?"

Barrios looked surprised. "Do to them? You make it sound like I'm asking you to be complicit in ambushing your people. The last thing Mr. San Roman needs is for the US military to declare war on him. No, no. He wants your warning so he can avoid contact. The fewer Americans that know about this, the better it is for everyone. No one gets hurt, and everyone gets what they want."

Tate reluctantly admitted to himself that this was a deal he could live with. The current plan to re-settle South America was to move along the north coast and east, a path moving away from San Roman; it was only a fluke that Tate and his squad were there at all.

There was little risk of the US military stumbling into San Roman's sand box, but that did little to silence the voice in Tate's head that said what he was about to agree to was wrong. Justified, yes, but wrong.

Dante reached his hand across the table to Tate, who looked at it as demons and saints battled inside him.

Tate's expression hardened, as he made his decision and shook Dante's hand.

When he got back to his quarters, Tate checked the secure phone he'd been given by the colonel.

Hewett had called, leaving a message for Tate to call him back.

"I read your mission report," the colonel growled. "Is this some kind of joke?"

Tate couldn't tell if he sounded more angry or worried. "No, sir. That's what happened."

"An enemy special ops team. On our soil? I know it's been a long time since anyone's shot at you. Details get blurred in combat. You probably ran into some scavengers. We know they're organized and well equipped. I see reports all the time of contact with them, stripping whatever they find and selling it on the black market. Some of them must have seen you as a prime opportunity for a good haul. I'm glad you didn't take any casualties, but damn, Tate, the fact is you've been out of special operations for too long. You're rusty and got caught with your pants down. It happens. There's no shame in it."

Tate heard the colonel sigh and papers rustling. "I'm sending back your report before anyone else sees it and questions if you're the right man for this project. Your revised report will state your team made minor contact with a gang of scavengers. Okay, Jack?"

"But colonel..."

"Do you understand me, Sergeant Major?" said the colonel, with contained anger; it was more a statement than a question.

The sudden flare of temper hinted to Tate that he was close to a nerve. He paused as he considered what he was about to say; no matter what happened next, it would be a game changer. The only question was whether that change included painting a giant target on his back.

To hell with it, he thought. It was time to kick over this anthill and see who crawled out.

"Sir, we have one of the men who attacked us... and I'm going to find out everything he knows."

There was a long silence on the other end of the phone, and even though the colonel hadn't said anything, Tate sensed a palpable change in him.

"Damn it, Jack. I'm warning you now, you don't want to do this."

The colonel sounded more worried than dangerous. If he was keeping any secrets, now was Tate's moment to hit him while he was off balance, and he wound up to deliver a haymaker.

"I know there's a leak in my team. I'm pretty damn sure it was your organization that ambushed us at the villa. I'm going to squeeze this guy to a pulp until I find out who and why. Do you want to tell me where you fit into all of this, or do I find out from my prisoner?"

"Well..." sighed the colonel. "At the moment it looks like I'm in the middle of a shit-candle that's burning at both ends."

"Did you have anything to do with the ambush?"

"No," said the colonel flatly.

"I think it's time you told me what you know, sir."

"It doesn't sound like I have much choice," said the colonel. "But you're not going to like it. The outbreak did a lot more damage to our country than many know. All our systems of government, business, hell, even the military were fractured, and we lost a lot of men and women in power that kept things running. The vacuum was filled with amateurs. Some saw an opportunity to help their country, but others saw a chance for a quick rise to power. Now our country is infested with parasites who are feeding off this country, and slowly bleeding it out. I didn't spend my life serving this country only to sit back now and do nothing."

"And that's why you got involved with this...?"

"Ring. At least that's what they call themselves," said the colonel. "They said they were looking for patriots who wanted to stop what's happening to the country. They recruit powerful and influential members in the government, military, businesses, you name it. The plan was to operate outside the red tape and bureaucracy that's dragging down our country's ability to rebuild itself.

"But something was wrong. The principals the Ring was supposed to operate by began to change. It was small things at first, but then it got worse. In the beginning, our meetings, planning sessions, all of it was done in the open for everyone to have a voice, but over time people started having closed door meetings. Then I started hearing about off book operations. A new agenda was happening behind the scenes. I was recruited into the Ring by a trusted friend. I discovered he had his own concerns when one night he comes out of the shadows as I'm heading for my car. Scared the hell out of me. He said we've been lied to. Everything we've been doing is a smokescreen. There's something deeper, darker going on. That's all he would tell me. He was getting out and urged me to do the same, before it was too late."

With each new piece of the colonel's story, Tate weighed its validity, because sooner or later he'd have to make a decision if the colonel could be trusted.

"What did you do? Did you get out?"

"I was making plans to," said the colonel. "Disappear, cover my tracks. I wasn't sure how bad the threat was." His voice took on a steely resolve Tate had heard in his own voice when he had faced live or die situations.

"But then they killed my friend. They made it look like an accidental car wreck, but I saw the police report. Drunk. Driving too fast, lost control and wrapped his car around a tree in the middle of the night. Bullshit. He didn't drink, and he didn't drive at night because of his bad eyesight. They killed him. That changed everything. Instead of running, I decided I'm going to rip this organization a new asshole."

"What else should I know?" asked Tate.

"Enough that you don't want to get tangled up in any of this. There's something monumentally bad going on, and they're not messing around. If they suspect you're a threat, or even a hint they can't trust you, they'll come after you, Jack. You're on their radar as a good little soldier. You don't want to mess that up. I can't explain what happened at the villa. Maybe there's rival infighting in the Ring. Maybe it was a redundancy in case you couldn't handle it. I don't know, but if they wanted you dead, we wouldn't be having this conversation. My advice is to keep your head down."

Tate knew there was no way he could swallow the idea of playing a pawn just to save his own skin. He thought he'd have more time to consider his next move, but the time for a decision landed in front of him sooner than he had expected.

Could Hewett be trusted, or was he feeding Tate disinformation, hoping to play him like a puppet?

Ultimately, the answer didn't matter. Tate swore an oath to defend the constitution against all enemies, foreign *and domestic* and he would make a deal with the devil to do it.

It was time to make the deal; only time would tell if Hewett was the devil.

"I know too much to play dead, Colonel. In fact, I think your odds of success look a whole lot better if you added a 'boots on the ground' element to your course of action."

"Damn, Sergeant Major. Single handedly killed six well-trained operators, and now volunteering for covert ops? You aren't the man I met at the Orchid."

"A lot's happened," said Tate.

"That's an understatement, but glad to have you. Now look, at the moment I don't have much actionable intel. Over time, I'll work my way into their operation. As I find out more, we'll take these bastards apart one bone at a time. The success of the villa mission made you a viable asset to them. They'll begin to trust you on more important missions, and we'll use the intel you collect against them, but you have to be careful. They aren't shy about keeping eyes on you."

"Like Cooper?" said Tate. "I'll handle that leak, but if I'm going to be facing units like the one I ran into at the ambassador's villa, that'll be a problem. My team barely held it together in that last encounter. They don't have the combat experience. I need something more. An equalizer."

"There may be something I can do to level that playing field," said the colonel. "Give me some time to get back to you. Anything else?"

Tate was encouraged by the colonel's willingness. He wasn't convinced he could trust him, but it weighed in his favor.

"Yes. That file you have on the Night Devils. I need an address."

12

ENEMY WITHIN

Tate's guts were twisting inside him, aided with a generous helping of shame and anxiety. It had started the moment the plane's tires had met tarmac with a screech, at the Ronald Regan Washington National airport; and it hadn't let up since.

Tate was returning to his former life; the thing he'd convinced himself would never happen, could never happen, and here he was.

The discovery of Cooper leaking classified intel was compelling enough for Tate to agree to a deal with Dante Barrios, but as he pieced together the deeper implications of somebody planting a spy in his unit, he was mocked by the question of what he could do about it. He had no resources, no tools; when he walked away from his previous life, he'd cut all ties with anyone who could help him.

Dante would be bringing his prisoner to a secluded location for Tate in four days. The fact was that no matter what the captured soldier told Tate, he was utterly alone and feebly incapable to determine if he was lying, or act on what he believed. For two days, he'd racked his brain for a solution, refusing to acknowledge the harsh truth.

There was only one place he could turn to; the answer was in the folder on the seat next to Tate. Inside was a dossier on each member of the Night Devils he'd gotten from Colonel Hewett months before, at the Blue Orchid. Each of the Devils had a specialty, and Kaiden Benedict had the skills Tate needed so desperately he would swallow his disgrace to get it.

Tate looked out the window of the gypsy cab as it rolled down Arlington Boulevard. Stretches of houses were dotted with empty lots, piled with rubble and debris; dark reminders of panic and martial law.

When the outbreak hit, cities across the country began to fall as political correctness and politics crippled the ability for police and National Guard to take action; the President made the decision that would not happen to Washington DC. Martial Law was announced, even as armored vehicles sped throughout the city. The public was ordered to go home and stay there, with a blunt warning that beginning the next day at 6 AM anyone seen outside would be held at a detention facility indefinitely.

Emergency broadcasts instructed who to contact for medical aid and other special circumstances. Neighborhoods were given zone designations, and supplied with a schedule when food would be distributed on a weekly basis.

Initially there were some who saw the martial law as an opportunity for looting and anti-government protests. A melting pot of hundreds gathered at the Washington monument, from accusations of a power-hungry government running wild, demands the President be impeached to an open cry to over throw of the country.

The National Guard and police were ordered to keep a distance, but to use reasonable force if the protest turned into a riot.

A school bus of protesters was racing down an empty 15th Street, eager to join the rally, but unknown and unnoticed was that one of their group, Greg, had been bitten the night before while fighting off what he thought was a drunk as he and his buddies looted the local Starbucks.

Among all the cheering and yelling in the bus, nobody noticed the infection take their friend. Then the nightmare of dominos began to fall.

The bus driver didn't notice when the cheers and yells turned to shouts of alarm as he quickly crossed Constitution Avenue. He heard the screams a moment before the things that had been his friends reached around the driver's seat and tore open his chest.

His momentarily lifeless body slumped forward, with his dead weight putting the gas pedal to the floor. The three National Guardsmen's attention was on the mass of people shouting over each other with bullhorns, and didn't see the bus behind them wildly swerve and jump the sidewalk.

The radioed warning from another Guard unit came too late. The impact on the heavy armored Humvee crushed in the soft nose of the bus, driving the chassis down into the ground. Like a pole vault, the sudden stopping of the bus's kinetic energy transferred to the rear, causing the bus to cartwheel over the wrecked Humvee.

The thin skin of the bus was no match for the sudden shearing force, and it blew apart near its apex, catapulting the writhing corpses within into the crowded rally.

The news helicopter caught the entire thing on camera, as the dead savagely turned on the living in what the horrified reporter described as a "feeding frenzy of sharks". The expression was forever burned into the country's psyche.

Later, hearings would fail to determine if an order was given or if the soldiers panicked, but one after another the armored vehicles opened fire.

Up until the first .50 caliber machine gun began thumping out rounds, hardly anyone actually believed the National Guard had loaded weapons.

Soon, every soldier and cop with a weapon was pouring fire into the crowd. Few protesters survived both the 'sharks' and the bullets; it was a tragic, sickening event that would divide the nation. What many called a massacre was the cities narrow escape from an extinction event.

That night, the President addressed the country, speaking his own words; his spin-doctors had been given the night off. Ashen and red eyed, he did what few presidents had done before. He took every truth he knew about the rally and the outbreak, and dropped it squarely in the people's lap.

Any fantasy or denial the country held about the outbreak was swept away. The President announced a mandatory quarantine for the entire city of Washington DC. He explained the risk of infection was so dangerous and could spread so rapidly he had issued a 'shoot on sight' order to the National Guard. Anyone they saw would be considered infected, and a danger to everyone.

Additionally, a hotline was created for people to report sightings of anyone outside, or other suspicious activity.

That same night, Miss. Ala Vance called the hotline when she'd heard screaming from the house next door. When the National Guard arrived at the house, their knock at the door was met by snarls, growls and scratching at the door. Any doubt that the sounds were coming from a family dog were removed as a ragged hand clawed through the solid wood front door. The order was given, and the house and everyone inside was annihilated. Nobody was taking chances anymore.

Today, Washington DC was as close to normal as could be. Quick-fab walls were assembled, and safe zones were sectioned off. As other areas were secured, the zones were expanded, until little by little they joined up.

Now, people went to work, shopped, sent their kids to school, but nobody forgot what was hunting them somewhere beyond the walls.

The cab slowed down as it neared its destination, nudging Tate out of his own thoughts.

He got out and gave the driver an extra ten dollars to stick around, just in case things didn't go well.

It was a modest brick house with gabled windows on the second floor. Tate noticed a single car in the driveway as he came to the door.

A swarm of scenarios flooded Tate's mind, each one predicting what would happen in the next moments. He willed them all into silence.

He made his decision to be here, and had his reasons. Doubt had its chance to talk him out of it and lost; come what may, he was here.

Just as he was about to knock, the door opened.

Kaiden Benedict stood in the doorway, looking at Tate as if she were watching paint drying.

"You look like shit, Jack." She left him at the door and walked inside. "Come on," she said over her shoulder. "I have dinner on the table."

During the next twenty minutes, Kaiden had chatted with Tate like they'd seen each other last week.

He listened, while absorbing the moment. Except for her eyes, Kaiden didn't look like she'd aged at all. Her familiar ponytail was gone, but in typical Kaiden low-maintenance fashion, she went with a relaxed chin-length bob cut. On his way through the living room, he'd noticed the medals and trophies for several triathlons, mud runs and other endurance competitions. Her athletic build, tenacious will power and keen intelligence got her through the nine grueling months training for Marine Corps Forces, Special Operations Command.

When she joined the Night Devils, the men traded looks of unspoken skepticism, but their first mission said everything about her they needed to know. The men never gave her special treatment, and she never asked for it. No matter the miles, weight of a fully loaded combat pack or other demands of a mission, she pulled her own and was accepted as one of the team.

Her specialty in the team was intel analysis, and she was unsettlingly good at it.

Years before, the team had exhausted its resources in trying to determine the location of a high value target. Shortly after Kaiden joined the team, she requested the team do a recon of suspected areas the target could be hiding.

They spent the early winter cris-crossing a large rural area in southern Belarus. It was early morning as they drove down a country road, and while there was a light snow flurry, they could easily see the countryside.

They had just come to an old stone bridge when Kaiden had them stop the car. She told them the target was at the farm they'd passed a couple of miles back.

They returned on foot to scout the farm from a safe distance, so they wouldn't be seen.

There was nothing remarkable about the farm. Green acreage surrounded the white two-story farmhouse. Nearby was a feed silo and well kept red barn, with a tractor and other equipment parked next to it. Sheep grazed all around the house, while cattle dotted further in the distance.

The team scrutinized the farm from their vantage point, but saw nothing to indicate their target was inside.

"The sheep," said Kaiden, with a tired sigh.

"Those sheep?" said Tate. "Like the same sheep every other farm we've seen has?"

"How did you trigger jockeys ever complete a mission without me?" Kaiden asked.

The other team members only stared at her without a response.

"As far back as 1700 BC, the wealth of cities were built on the wool trade. That's why, even now, sheep farmers are more protective of their livestock than any other types of farmers."

"Thanks for the history lesson," said Tate. "How about connecting the dots for us trigger jockeys?"

"I only mention it because wool is what those sheep don't have. Those sheep have been sheared, something farmers only do in midsummer, never in winter, which could kill them. They also wouldn't leave expensive equipment like that tractor out in the snow. It would be in the barn."

Tate looked at the farm through his binoculars, then back at Kaiden. "That's it? You think our target's there because a farmer's got bad timing and doesn't put his toys away?"

Kaiden smiled, accepting Tate's challenge. "Our target's highly allergic to lanolin, which is found where? Wool. He travels with two custom-built armored cars, a Land Rover Defender for his guards, and a Mercedes S Class for himself. Not the kind of things that blend into rural countryside. He'd have to hide them in the barn, which wouldn't leave any room for the farmers equipment. Last, but not least, a nice two-story farmhouse leaves lots of room for a farmer's family, a high profile target... and his guards, don't you think?"

Tate reluctantly agreed to set up surveillance of the farmhouse, and three days later they saw their target through an upstairs window.

From that day forward, Kaiden would use her ability to interpret meaning out of the meaningless. She was so good it was spooky, and earned her the call sign Nostradamus, or Nos for short.

Tate returned from his reminiscing to find Kaiden looking at him, slightly annoyed.

"Am I boring you?" she asked.

He'd been lost in thought, and didn't know how long she'd been staring at him. For a moment, he'd forgotten where he was and his purpose for being there.

"No. Sorry, it's just that this is..."

"Not what you expected," said Kaiden.

"Under the circumstances I didn't know what to expect, least of all that you'd have dinner set for me."

"Give me a little credit, Jack. Your kid died while you were deployed on a mission. You blamed yourself for not protecting her, and after emotionally whipping yourself raw, you decided you weren't any good to anyone and left. That about sum it up?"

Tate only sat looking baffled. In a few words, she had just unraveled the tangled mess he'd lived through and all the complexities of his emotions with the simplicity of untying a shoelace.

"When you put it that way it sounds..."

"Like it makes sense?" finished Kaiden. "Yeah, it makes sense. It was also selfish and a bullshit move."

She tipped her bottle and finished off her beer, then got up from the table and brought in a box from the other room. She put it in front of Tate, and gave him a devilish smile.

"After you're done doing the dishes, I'll be in the living room. You can tell me what you want me to do."

Curious, Tate opened the box. A surge of mixed emotions flooded through him as he recognized his old gear. His hand moved under its own power as he took out a classic Colt 1911 pistol.

The .45 had been with him in countless operations, and in spite of advancements in pistols, he refused to carry anything else.

As a boy, Tate had read the exploits of the WWI hero, Sergeant York, and how he'd defeated an entire squad of charging Germans with nothing but his Colt .45 1911. Pirates could keep their swords, Robin Hood could have his bow, but young Jack Tate promised himself that one day he'd wear a Colt.

He puzzled over why Kaiden had saved his things; it was a question that, for the moment, would have to wait.

Tate and Kaiden talked late into the night. For most of it, Kaiden listened quietly, letting Tate exhaust all the information he had; the mission to the villa, the captured soldier, Cooper leaking information, and the possibility that Colonel Hewett might be involved.

It was nearly 2:30 AM when he finished. He sat back in his seat, feeling tired, and waited for Kaiden to reveal the answers he couldn't find.

She stood up and walked to the stairs. "Give me thirty minutes to get ready. Something big is going on, but there's too many missing pieces still. Let's peel someones fingernails off and see what we learn."

Tate felt exhausted and sluggish. He wanted nothing more than to stretch out on the couch for a few hours, but that would have to wait.

He had a meeting to keep with Dante Barrios, and his prisoner. Tate felt relief that Kaiden had been so quick to accept his return, and willing to help. He couldn't help but suspect she knew more about what he'd up to the past couple of years than she was saying.

"By the way, how did you know I was coming here? I mean, you even had dinner ready."

Kaiden paused at the bottom of the stairs and smiled at him. "A girl's got to have her secrets, right?"

Tate would have to live with that answer for now, but he knew there was more to it, and it would nag at him until he found out.

He caught himself smiling as he wondered about the recent events. Four hours ago, he thought he'd be on a flight back home with a broken jaw and empty handed. Instead, he had a highly-skilled member of the Night Devils.

Tate sat in a beat up folding chair, in an abandoned auto body shop. A few feet across from him was Dante's prisoner; the enemy soldier with his feet and hands flex-cuffed to the chair.

Kaiden leaned against the wall off to the side but was close enough to hear the conversation.

Tate and Kaiden could easily see that San Roman's men had beaten the soldier bloody. His close-cropped hair revealed dried blood from a large gash on his scalp. The skin on his face was split open in several places, and his nose had been broken, yet it was clear by his straight posture and direct eye contact his spirit wasn't broken. His uniform was dirty and torn. There was no name tab or indication of rank.

Tate sensed the soldier's defiance almost daring them to beat him for answers.

"I'm Jack Tate. You said you have some information for me."

The soldier looked from Tate to Kaiden, seeking an explanation.

"She's with me," said Tate.

Satisfied, the prisoner relaxed.

"Who are you, and why did you ask for me?"

The prisoner tilted his head towards his bound wrists. "Do you mind?"

There was nothing within his arms reach, and it was doubtful he could take on both of them in a fight.

There was a glint of steel as Kaiden flicked open a knife. She walked behind the prisoner and cut the thick plastic ties around his wrists.

He waited until Kaiden had put some distance between them before he moved his arms.

"My name is Nathan," he said, massaging his wrists. "Why did I ask for you? Because I knew if I could provide you with something of value you could do the same for me."

Tate's chair creaked as he leaned back, and considered what Nathan had just said. "I'm listening."

"You have a leak in your team," said Nathan.

"Yeah, I got your message through Barrios," said Tate. "I know who the leak is."

"But you don't understand why there's a leak, or how it's all connected."

"You seem to know a lot for a grunt," said Tate.

Nathan tried to smile, but the pain of his split lip and bruised face reduced him to a grimace.

"Yes and no. Had my vocation been combat, like the rest of my team, I would have escaped with them when we were ambushed by San Roman's guerrillas. If I knew as much about tactical withdrawals as intelligence analysis, I wouldn't be here. I was there to assess those documents you took from the villa, and report back to my people."

"What people are those?" asked Tate.

"My People," said Nathan, with a smile. "My employers, to be accurate. As you might have guessed, I'm an independent businessman."

Considering he looked, and likely felt like he'd been trampled by a stampede of cement trucks, Nathan came across like he was having a casual conversation with friends at a dinner party. If he was worried or nervous, he was hiding it very well.

"But, let me get to the point. I don't see a future in the hands of Mr. San Roman. I imagine he's using me as a bargaining chip to make a deal with you, and once you've agreed to that deal, which I'm guessing you have because you're here, he'll kill me."

Tate could feel Kaiden's eyes shift from Nathan to him. He didn't tell Kaiden anything about a deal, and now with that piece of information exposed, Tate could hear the wheels turning in her head.

He knew better than keeping her in the dark, but it was a detail about his situation that he had wanted to keep to himself.

Tate mentally kicked himself for screwing up. He'd have to come clean with her and stop keeping things close to his vest.

"Yeah. They'll probably kill you right after we leave," said Tate. "Tough break."

"My thoughts exactly," said Nathan. "And it's why I asked for you to begin with. If you were to take me with you when you leave here I would, in return, use my access to my employer's intel regarding your situation."

"Or we could break you out and you disappear," said Kaiden. "We never hear from you again."

"Then you'd know as much as if San Roman had killed me," smiled Nathan. "Nothing ventured, nothing gained. This isn't about trust, it's about risk and reward. Weigh the risk of me reneging on our deal against the value of the reward, and getting a peek at the other guy's cards. What I know at the moment is my employers see the fragility of your government as an opportunity."

The hairs rose up on the back of Tate's neck. "If anyone sends their army to invade, America will have them returned in body bags," he growled.

Nathan leaned forward, and fixed Tate with a grave stare. "Oh no, not to invade. To infiltrate."

Dante Barrios' surprise when he saw Nathan walk out in the company of Tate and Kaiden suddenly turned to fear, when he found himself looking down the barrel of Tate's Colt 1911.

"I'm making a small change to our original deal," said Tate.

"San Roman will not react well to this," said Dante.

Tate pressed the barrel of his gun to Dante's forehead. "You really want to tell your boss you let me just walk out of here with your prisoner? Sure, he'll be mad at me, but what do you think he'll do to the messenger?"

Tate gave Dante a moment to let the thought sink in.

"Talk about a career ender. One way or another, you were going to kill this guy anyway, so tell San Roman you dumped his body and that's that. I get what I want, and you get to keep living."

"You make a convincing point," said Dante. "We have an agreement."

Tate put his gun away, knowing that Kaiden had her hand on her gun just out of sight of Dante. Any shadow of a suspicious movement on his part, and he'd be dead an instant later.

Tate grinned inwardly, thinking how good it felt to have someone he could count on again.

13

CLEANING HOUSE

C ooper sat in the low dirt trench, bored and indifferent to the distant gunfire.

He'd pulled go-fer duty on the rifle range, replacing targets while the rest of his team was 400 meters away, practicing their shooting skills.

Each motorized target would dip below the dirt berm on a random pattern, making it more challenging for the shooters. Cooper sat in a trench that ran the width of the gun range, and connected to each target station.

The plywood board over his head kept the full brutality of the sun off of him, but also blocked any breeze that could have helped.

As the drops of sweat dripped off his nose, he wondered how the human race survived before air conditioning.

He flinched as a bullet smacked into the protective earthen berm above him, and a trickle of dirt ran into the trench.

He snatched up the radio, crushing the talk button. "You assholes! Stop doing that." Even from this distance, he could hear them laughing.

"Oops," Rosse chuckled over the radio. "Did that hit near you?"

"You know damn well it did," shouted Cooper.

The boredom, heat and buzzing flies had eaten through his

patience, and although he knew the trench was keeping him safe from the bullets, it rattled him when they hit near him.

"Cease fire, cease fire, cease fire," said Tate over the radio. "Cooper, replace the targets. Everyone else take a twenty-minute break. Leave your weapons on the bench. Remove the magazines and lock your bolts open. Cooper, target three is stuck in down position. See what you can do."

"Okay, Top," said Cooper. He got up from his bench and followed the trench towards target three.

He thought it strange he hadn't seen the sergeant major since they'd returned from the villa mission. There was talk around the base that he'd left for a while, and came back with a woman. Nobody knew who she was, or what she was doing here; Cooper couldn't decide if he felt more, or less nervous about the sergeant major's absence.

Cooper stopped at target three. A simple design, the target was nothing more than a five by four foot board, on a tall board that was raised and lowered by a chain and gear system. The motor was inside a shallow room, dug into the berm just beneath the target. The brilliant sunlight cast the motor room in dark shadow.

Cooper stood at the black entrance, and swore under his breath as he realized he hadn't brought his flashlight.

Just as he turned to go back for it, a hand shot out of the darkness of the motor room and yanked him into the gloom.

It happened so fast there was no time to yelp. In the blackness, he felt himself spun around, then slammed into a rough earthen wall.

Stunned and blind, he didn't know if he should run or fight.

Suddenly, a blinding light stabbed him in the eyes. The light moved out of this eyes and he blinked away the dots, to see Sergeant Major Tate's scowling face inches from his.

The flashlight threw distorted shadows over Tate's face, making him more ghoul than human.

Cooper's eyes were wide with terror. Something glinted in the beam of light, and Cooper froze as he felt the hairline edge of a knife press into his throat.

Tate leaned in closer, speaking in a low snarl. "One chance to talk, or I'll slit you from ear to ear."

The blade of the knife was pressing against his throat so hard, Cooper was sure if he swallowed he'd cut his own throat, but every second of silence marched him closer to death.

"It was me, but I didn't want to. They forced me."

"Who? Who are *they*?" demanded Tate.

"I don't know. Please don't kill me. Please! I only spoke to one guy. Mr. Red. He told me what to do. I had to," pleaded Cooper. "I never met anyone face to face."

Menace pulsed off of Tate in waves. "How did he contact you?"

Terrified of moving, Cooper indicated his breast pocket by looking at it. "The phone in my pocket. That's all I know. He'd tell me what to do, and I had to do it. I'm sorry, Top. I'm so sorry."

Tate took the phone out of Cooper's pocket, and put it in his. "What do you mean, had to?"

"They took my family. Chopped off my baby sister's finger and mailed it to me. He told me worse would happen if I didn't obey them." Cooper's sorrow for his family overtook his fear of the knife at his throat, as tears spilled down his cheeks.

For a long moment, Tate's expression didn't change, and Cooper knew there'd soon be a rasping sharp pain across his throat. He would try to breathe, but it would only be a gurgle and he would drown in his own blood, but then Cooper heard someone whispering near Tate.

Tate's gaze broke from Cooper, and the flashlight went out.

Cooper stayed frozen in place, surrounded in the blackness. Miraculously, he felt the knife leave his throat.

Before he could breathe a sigh of relief the room light was switched on, partially blinding Cooper.

As his vision adjusted, he saw the sergeant major and a woman he'd never seen before.

"Hi," said Kaiden brightly. "Rough day, huh? The good news is, we've decided your terminal discharge from the military is premature. For the time being, you're going to stay on base like nothing's happened. You're not going to talk to anyone about this, right?"

Cooper could breathe again. He wasn't going to die, but it gave him no comfort. There was something about this woman that scared him; he was sure her smile would be the same if she kissed you or killed you.

"Nobody. I'll stay right here. I mean, you know, not here in this room, but..."

Kaiden smiled at Tate and patted him on the shoulder. "There, you see? He won't be any trouble."

Tate put his knife back in the sheath, and tossed Cooper's phone to Kaiden. "Can you use this?"

Kaiden turned on the phone and tapped a few buttons. "It's encrypted, but a piece of junk. I'll be able to reverse-track any numbers on the call history."

Tate looked at her with a mixture of astonishment and disbelief. "Since when can you do that?" he asked.

"Hey, just because you let yourself go to pot," she said, "doesn't mean the rest of us have." She dropped the phone in her pocket and headed for the door, with Tate following her.

"Hey, wait," said Cooper. "What happens now?"

Tate stopped and looked over his shoulder at the sweat-soaked Cooper. "You mean am I going to kill you, or let you live? You'll get my answer in a couple of days, unless you run. Then I'll kill you."

Tate walked out, leaving Cooper in the agony of an unknown future.

―――――

The Black Hawk helicopter thudded over the muted green of the jungle, as the sun edged into the dusk. It banked steeply over the ruined carcass of a small village.

Rotting corpses, which had lain undisturbed, rose to their feet craning their sunken, milky eyes to the sound of the machine above them. As the helicopter retreated, they moved with renewed purpose, trailing behind it.

Inside the helicopter, Tate and Kaiden sat across from each other, with a squirming body bag on the floor between them.

"Just like old times," smiled Kaiden.

The crew chief looked dubiously from Tate to the moving body bag and back.

"Like I said, Chief, it's a training mission."

"Whatever you say, Sergeant Major," said the crew chief, with a shrug.

It had been three days since he and Kaiden had questioned Cooper at the gun range, and grim satisfaction had replaced the anger Tate had been feeling before; he didn't like loose ends, and this was one Tate was about to sew up.

Tate took an envelope out of his pocket and handed it to Kaiden, who looked at him with mild curiosity.

"What's this?" she asked as she opened it.

"We finally got our new unit designation," said Tate.

Kaiden scanned the document, and handed it back to Tate with a wry smile. "I like the name. Your idea, right?"

"It seemed like a good fit," said Tate.

A few minutes later, the Black Hawk flared over a clearing and settled down in the tall grass. Tate hopped out of the cargo compartment, followed by Kaiden.

"We'll be back in thirty minutes," said Tate.

The crew chief gave a thumbs up in response.

Tate grabbed the end of the body bag and pulled it across the deck, then hefted it over his shoulder.

Tate and Kaiden walked into the murky jungle.

They'd gone a few hundred yards, when they stopped near a tree with low limbs.

Tate dumped the body bag from his shoulder. It landed with a thud. Something inside grunted in pain.

Kaiden took off her pack and pulled a coil of rope from it. With an easy fling, she threw the end of the rope over a tree limb, ten feet above.

Tate unzipped the body bag, revealing a hooded figure inside. The figure was flex cuffed at the wrists and ankles.

Kaiden looped the rope around the cuffs and tied a knot.

Together, she and Tate hoisted the other end of the rope, pulling the figure to their feet; the figure wobbled briefly before gaining their balance.

Back at the base, Cooper's empty room was dark. His cell phone lay on the bed. The phone began to beep, and the display lit up: *Caller ID: Unknown.* It beeped several times, but there was no one to answer it.

Kaiden took a sack out of her backpack and removed a bell with a length of chain attached to it, then wrapped the other end of the chain around the ankle of the hooded figure.

Tate fished a knife out of her bag and pushed the handle into the hands of the bound figure.

"Hang on to that," said Tate. "It's the only thing that can save you, because after what you've done, I sure as hell won't."

Cooper's phone stopped beeping, and lay quiet and inanimate as if it had never made a sound. Darkness rushed in to fill the void left by the bright display.

Tate looked at his watch and nodded to himself. "About time to finish this up."

He picked up the slack rope and began pulling on it, lifting the hooded figure off the ground until the bell swung freely under his feet.

The figure's protests were muffled beneath the hood.

Tate tied the rope off around a short but stout tree, and walked back to stand in front of the hooded figure.

"After we leave, you can either hang here until your hands rot off, or you can try to cut yourself down. If you choose the latter, every step you take will ring that bell. Since we stirred up a lot of those undead eating machines not too far from here... well, few sounds carry like a clanging bell. Personally, I've seen what those things have done to people. Laying there, watching your limb ripped off and eaten in front of you is a hard way to go. Maybe you'll decide to open a vein with that knife before they get to you. Either way, I don't care. We're done here."

The hooded figure's yells were nothing more than muffled sounds, but it was clear they were trying to say something.

Tate reached up and pulled off the hood, then pulled the wadded up sock out of the figure's mouth.

The quiet of Cooper's room was broken as his cell phone began beeping. The same unknown caller ID was on the display.

Footsteps ran up and stopped outside the door. Keys jangled as someone dropped them on the floor.

The phone kept beeping, taunting someone to reach it before it fell silent again.

The doorknob rattled and light flooded into the room from the hallway.

Cooper ran to the bed and snatched up the phone. "Hello? Hello? Mr. Red? I'm sorry, I was..."

A soft, young voice came over the phone. "Big brother? Is that you?"

All strength left Cooper's legs, and he sat heavily on the floor. "Julie? Sis, is that you? Is everyone okay? How did you get this number?"

Tate looked into the terror-filled eyes of the man strung up in front of him.

"My time's running short, Mr. Red. If you have something to tell me, make it fast," said Tate.

"I was just doing my job," pleaded Mr. Red, as he tried to keep his voice from trembling.

"Like cutting that little girl's finger off?" asked Kaiden. "That part of your job, too?"

Mr. Red's eyes darted between Tate and Kaiden, searching for any sign of clemency, but only finding cold resolve.

"I've told you everything I know. But... but I could help you. Be a resource like a... an inside guy."

In the distance, they could hear the whine of the Black Hawk turbines spinning up.

"If we could use Cooper's phone to track you down, in spite of those amateur encoded repeaters, just think of what we can do with your computer, cell phone, all those files we took from your apartment," said Kaiden. "Don't get me wrong. If it was up to me, I'd love to have you on the team, but Jack's got trust issues, okay? Okay. Bye-bye."

She picked up the dirt-covered sock Tate had dropped, and stuffed it back into Mr. Red's mouth as he began to sob pitifully.

She shouldered her backpack and headed towards the sound of the helicopter.

Tate paused a moment longer, looking at the hanging man's terrified eyes. "Don't give up, Red. There's a least a five percent chance you'll get out of this alive, and if you do, and you make it back to your friends, tell them the Grave Diggers are coming for them."

The End

YOUR REVIEW HELPS

Thank you for reading The Grave Diggers.

Reviews are a huge support for a self published author, like yours truly. If you enjoyed this book, please leave a review and tell your friends about my books.

You can leave your review here

ENJOY THIS FREE BOOK

Add this free prequel to your library!

A simple mission turns into terrifying fight for survival.

This special forces team is about to walk into something more horrifying and relentless than they could ever imagine.

BOOKS IN THE SERIES

Is your Grave Diggers library complete?

―――――――――

The Grave Diggers

The Suicide King

Grave Mistakes

Deadly Relics

AUTHORS NOTE

Digging Into The Story

While reading this book you may have asked yourself, 'When did this happen? In the future, or is this a parallel world, or what?' You might (even) have gone back and reread some of it, thinking you missed the key sentence that explains it. To answer your (assumed) second question, no, this isn't a parallel world. In answer to your (equally assumed) first question the answer is *the near future*. I know. That doesn't exactly put a pin on a year, but if it's any help in narrowing down a date, you probably have enough time to work out your evacuation plan and stock up on MRE's before society is cannibalized by the undead.

I kept to current military gear because most equipment has a long service life before something new comes along. Look at the M14 rifle, for example. It first saw action in 1961 and is still in service 55 years later. I did cave to the temptation to come up with a fictitious weapon because, come on, it's cool.

One Last Thing

If you think you've seen all there is to the Vix in this book you'd be very mistaken. I've grown up on zombie lore and, like you, feel that once the monster has stepped out from behind the curtain you've seen it all. What kind of storyteller would I be if I did that to you? There's more to the Vix you haven't seen yet, and judging by how creeped out people got from reading the early copy of my next book, I think you'll enjoy it.

ABOUT THE AUTHOR

Chris grew up on George Romero, Rambo, Star Wars and Tom Clancy, a formula for a creating a seriously good range of science fiction, action, paranormal, and adventure novels.

Chris is currently working on The Grave Digger series, an action packed thrill ride that will have you hooked right up to the last page. It's Tom Clancy meets Dawn of the Dead and X-Files, and it's guaranteed to keep you on the edge of your seat. Jack Tate, ex-Delta operator, has assembled a rag-tag team of rookies and motley group of wannabes is all he has to go up against a secret cabal who are plotting a takeover of the United States. Can they do it before time runs out?

website: chrisfritschi.com

Printed in Great Britain
by Amazon